THE BOOK OF EVE

THE BOOK
OF EVE

CARMEN BOULLOSA

Translated by Samantha Schnee

DEEP VELLUM PUBLISHING

DALLAS, TEXAS

Deep Vellum Publishing
3000 Commerce St., Dallas, Texas 75226
deepvellum.org · @deepvellum

Deep Vellum is a 501c3 nonprofit literary arts organization
founded in 2013 with the mission to bring
the world into conversation through literature.

FIRST EDITION, 2023

Support for this publication was provided in part by grants from the National
Endowment for the Arts, Amazon Literary Partnership, the Texas Commission on the
Arts, City of Dallas Office of Arts & Culture, and the George & Fay Young Foundation.

 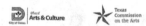

LIBRARY OF CONGRESS CATALOGING-IN-PUBLICATION DATA

Names: Boullosa, Carmen, author. | Schnee, Samantha, translator.
Title: The book of Eve / Carmen Boullosa ; translated by Samantha Schnee.
Other titles: Libro de Eva. English
Description: First edition. | Dallas, Texas : Deep Vellum Publishing,
[2023]
Identifiers: LCCN 2022056724 | ISBN 9781646052240 (trade paperback) | ISBN
9781646052509 (ebook)
Subjects: LCSH: Feminism--Fiction. | LCGFT: Novels.
Classification: LCC PQ7298.12.O76 L4513 2023 | DDC
863/.64--dc23/eng/20221202
LC record available at https://lccn.loc.gov/2022056724

ISBN (TPB) 978-1-64605-224-0
ISBN (Ebook) 978-1-64605-250-9

Cover design by In-House International Creative, weareinhouse.com | @weareinhouse

Interior layout and typesetting by KGT

PRINTED IN THE UNITED STATES OF AMERICA

To the memory of Psiche Hughes, my polestar, in celebration of the joy we shared, and her generous intelligence.

To Marisa Arango, because she was taken from me before her time.

To Ana Luisa Liguori, Magali Lara, Marta Lamas, Alicia Rodríguez, Lucía Melgar, María Teresa Priego, Merce Gómez, Giuliana Bruno, Betsy Sussler, Kim Baker, the two Raquels (Serur and Chang Rodríguez), and Marcela Rodríguez.

To my formidable Mike Wallace, my greatest source of strength, a much better companion than Adam was to Eve.

Every poem is a genesis.
Every new poem
memorizes the future.
Every poem is beginning.
                    —Eduardo Lizalde (paraphrased)

. . . knowledge is good,
And Life is good; and how can both be evil?
                    —Byron, *Cain*

The world begins at a kitchen table.
. . . Perhaps the world will end at a kitchen table,
while we are laughing and crying,
eating of the last, sweet bite.
                    —Joy Harjo

What follows is a transcription of private papers relating the deeds of Eve, which have been preserved for generations. The tale encompasses

the genesis of the universe,
woman in Eden,
the bite of the apple,
the voices of the trees,
the leaves of the speechless ficus,
Thunder and its crime,
the departure from Eden,
the taking of fire,
the discovery of Earth,
the cold,
the weeping,
the laughter,
the nights,
the desire to have children,
the arrival of Cain—
the farmer,
a comment on Eve's attempts at pottery,
the conception and birth of Abel,
his flock,
the bread,
the story of Adah,

the beer,
the offering or sacrifice imposed by Noah,
the fratricide,
the dream of the homunculi,
Eve's skiff,
the Tower of Babel,
among other well-known passages,
as well as other unknown ones,
such as the birth of the clitoris,
Adam's frustration and resentment,
the horse's progeny,
and how the penis came into being, after much exertion.

Other voices accompany that of Eve: those of her daughters—Adah and her sisters—interspersed between chapters, and the two voices of Cain (one from the Land of Nod), as well as that of Abel in the underworld, along with a few further annotations, anecdotes, and versions that differ from those that Eve proffers when she takes up the reins of this tale.

CONTENTS

The Book of Eve

Containing ten books in ninety-one parts

Accompanied by a selection of loose papers—differing
versions or those of others

You have been granted the privilege of receiving Eve's papers. If, upon reading them, you think they're not for you, give them to someone you deem appropriate. Take good care of them, they have been entrusted to you.

But if you appreciate them, when you feel your light diminishing, choose the personage of their next destination with great care and confidence. Do not hold on to them, risking their destruction.

The Letter

If your daughters do not heed you, if your friends and kin do not believe what you tell them, keep these books of Eve out of their hands. As soon as you are able, copy them and give them to someone you are sure will be their loyal guardian. And when you copy them, remember you should transfer them into your own tongue and manner of speaking. You must never allow Eve's voice to remain hidden in the past.

Loose paper from the books of Eve

Teresa of Avila's Prologue

They gave me a crude manuscript from Toledo. It purports to be a version of Genesis written by Eve.

They asked me to write about it. Here I shall tell what it entails:

It's an infuriating, absolutely outrageous text, because its pages do not acknowledge the righteousness, the majesty, the greatness of the Creator of all things.

Cursed pen, whoever wrote it did so to please the Devil. What wretched, feeble soul who, having lost their wits, was incognizant of the mercies and works of God before their very eyes.

The vulgarity of the vessel of this self-absorbed soul is astounding! Their blindness is an abomination. It's about nothing but bodies and desires, which are both servants of the soul, nothing but our God-given senses and powers.

The words herein are like a worm, so brimming with foul odor that its fetidness is repugnant to the very words themselves, as if one enters into sunshine, blinded by dirt.

Alas! So much wickedness, like serpents and vipers and other pernicious things.

It's sheer nonsense, illustrating the advanced illness of this soul in such deep misery that they speak of God as of the cruelest, most despotic master, most infamous among slaves.

The manuscript bears the imprimatur of one who is unredeemed by the blood of Christ, which is why the Son gave himself up, to redeem each and every one of us. It's besmirched by a nefarious being who refused Redemption. But even bearing that in mind, the voice that speaks herein—a voice so far from light, with its disturbed senses, ungoverned and deliberately deaf— treads blindly upon the path of hate and vengeance.

Wrought completely from the darkness they have sought, fallen into mortal sin, shut away in a place where there is no darkness more sinister, nor any blacker thing than this deformed soul itself, whoever wrote these words in the name of Eve is a filthy insect that instinctively and deliberately chose to veer from the righteous path in favor of poisonous, pestilent black waters.

Every single word that flows from this so-called Eve is a vessel of misfortune and filth.

She has no fear of offending the Creator. The Sun does not warm a single one of her works, let's not call them her words, but rather what she tells us she has done: thief of fire, creator of the very bowls that boiled the devil's bile, poisoning the victuals of her family, wanton, lost soul . . . She admits atrocities more vile than the most detestable of vices.

Let's forgive her madness, she's unimportant, a lost soul in service to the devil. Let's forgive her, just as divine Jesus will, when he recovers from his state of dejection, because surely, she provoked his Majesty as well.

Let's forgive her, but let's not listen to her. Let's remember that the Devil made her wicked, and that he likes to trick us with illusions. Let's just ignore her. Absorbed in her world, consumed by her pleasures, and lost in her ambitions, wherever the light of the Creator might have entered her there is nothing other than putrefaction, and he is reflected in all of his works, all that exists.

But enough. I refuse to dine at a trough in a pigsty, a pigpen, some den, some lair, some stable. I shall close my mouth, no evil spirit shall contaminate me with such unmitigated hogwash!

And in case anyone smells a rat, I have taken the liberty of using scissors and a knife to remove the tumor where it is stated that this Eve of whom the text speaks was a Negress. There's no better explanation for her nature!

Books One to Ten

in which Eve tells her story in different moods, according to which part of the story she's telling

BOOK ONE

1

The Beginning

Before me, all was Chaos, a vast disarray, endlessness, the turmoil of darkness and light, the heavens and the abyss, above and below, lightness and weight, water and earth. There was no one to witness this. Everything was amorphous, unfinished, pending. Everything burned wildly.

This pandemonium was magnificent in its own way.

I know something about Chaos. I didn't experience it firsthand, but Chaos is part of me. And I'm not alone in the Cosmos in that regard; Chaos is here today; its power animates the Universe.

Because of me, human pleasure and pain exist; and since I am the heir of Chaos, humans confuse pleasure and pain.

After Chaos, the Earth began to spin on its axis, creating gravity. But let's leave things there, because that transformation, that craziness, that sudden coming together, would take up this whole story. Let's spend our time on others:

Two sources of light pursued the Earth—the Sun and the Moon—a multitude of stars, comets, scattered asteroids, and other nameless heavenly bodies, some falling apart and spinning out of orbit without rhyme or reason. To be completely accurate, the Sun did not pursue the Earth, but in those times that's how it appeared and that's why it's written so here.

This perception wasn't foolish: our planet, enrobed in its atmosphere, was a thing of beauty to behold. But beauty and horror go hand in hand: the titans sprang forth from planet's core, responding to the call of the Moon and the Sun. They rebelled against Earth's internal pressure, just like geysers, spring waters, and volcanic eruptions.

The titans were misshapen, their very forms the image of Chaos. They were dim-witted shades, dumb, wandering shadows that moved slowly, relics of the early times with no reason for existence. Their deformity, and not their size, is how they got their name, because on Earth all living creatures were shaped harmoniously, except the short-lived titans.

The giants came next. I lived at the same time as them but can't say much about them, because only infants can see giants clearly, and I was never a child. From the beginning I was an adult, or whatever you call the age I am, ageless.

Legend has it that the giants were born of the titans. This is completely unfounded, because all those who preceded Eve bore no offspring; the titans died out, leaving no descendants. I was and still am the first to ever conceive offspring, whereas the titans and giants sprouted like seeds or erupted like volcanos. Before me, all creation was part of a chain reaction; giving birth started with me. Before me, Chaos and Eternity. Everything that came into being was motherless.

Alas, the Mother: she is the personification of creation, irruption, the presence of the dark tunnel that delivers us to life, and worse: the keeper of the seed, the one who gives nourishment, the one who provides. A terrible figure. She ought to be mistrusted, not celebrated, because she consumes us—and if you don't have your Mother's approval it's like being devoured twice over.

Over time, the giants had children with our own species. These were proud beings who disdained beauty; confident in their powers, they committed atrocities on par with those that some attributed to the giants.

And humans copulated with angels, too. The creatures produced by the union of women and angels settled in the first city, ruining Cain's dream, the same one Noah would later have: creating a race free from wickedness by shortening the lives of its inhabitants, because if they lived too long some would become wicked, discovering the pleasures of vice. I'll get to that story later.

The "tides" of Chaos—some of which were universal, others localized—were a formidable force, causing as much damage as war.

One of the last began near Earth, a little farther than the Moon. That was when Beelzebub, the greatest angel of all, fell from the heavens because of his arrogance, betraying his heavenly nature; it happened because of his attraction to the Earth, which made him anchor himself here as if he were one of us. Which was, of course, irreversible.

Though he himself was magnificent in his resplendence, Beelzebub could not restrain himself when faced with so much earthly beauty. He couldn't stand it; hungry and greedy, he wanted to devour everything he saw.

Chewing giddily, Beelzebub stuffed himself silly, acting such the glutton that he collapsed, falling into one of the circles of the underworld.

The Moon howled with laughter.

The Moon's long belly laugh shook the Earth and its surroundings. I wasn't there, I learned this much later: it was recorded on stone and in water's deference to the Moon.

The laughter of the Moon, magnificent in her defiance, gave Earth the constant of cold, lunar incandescence.

The Moon is, first and foremost, female (so they say), even in her fits of laughter. The same is true of Earth. And what is there that is not female? Tell me.

2

Presenting Eve, the Apple, Eden, and Eve's Daughters, Who Ask About the Serpent

I, Eve, am the first of our kind.

Everything began with what they call "the apple." The commonly accepted hypothesis about Adam and the clay and the breath is wrong—and I'm going to reveal its malicious origin. It is true that flesh, like the leaves on the trees, ribs, stones, and dirt, is made of stardust.

But asserting that the life-giving force worked with clay to create humans is false. Saying that man's flesh preceded mine and that mine was wrought from a rib is nonsense.

Our roots are not in the ground, they can be traced to a fruit.

My name is Eve. I have no past. I was born of no one. I had no childhood. I'm the being that never dies. The first. The mother of you all.

"*Despite Hell and its envy,*"[1] I, "*righter of wrongs, undoer of abuses,*"[2] will speak the truth here. Everything began with the bite I took of that fruit, the one they call "the apple" because their memories have been subjugated. It wasn't an apple. That's mere

---

1. "*A pesar del Infierno y de su envidia.*" Sor Juana Inés de la Cruz, "Villancico III," in *Obras Completas* (Mexico City: Porrúa, 2012). All translations by Samantha Schnee unless otherwise specified.
2. "*deshacedora de entuertos, destrozadora de injurias.*" Sor Juana Inés de la Cruz, "Villancico VI," *Obras Completas*.

nonsense. The creation of the apple was a time-consuming human endeavor—and still is: every harvest, every tree requires care, kindness, imagination, luck—and the first one was cultivated by Cain, "No knowledge is as precious as that which a child gives its mother." Sweet Cain, whom I nicknamed "Seeds," my farmer son.

In Eden there was no such thing as "care," "kindness," "imagination," or "luck." In Eden, fruits, legumes, seeds, leaves, greens, and vegetables had no flavor or scent. Like everything else, fruit grew from stardust; it was luck that made it delicious.

From that moment luck became an inseparable companion of mine, of ours. It wasn't the only thing that the "apple" gave us.

It's also untrue that I did not bite the apple, as has been written elsewhere (*she didn't care if Adam took a bite / she did not taste it*).[3] I did bite the apple; why would I deny it, when I'm proud of it? It's slanderous drivel to say that in doing so I committed the "original sin."

The delicious fruit awakened my senses. I smelled a scent for the first time.

My sense of smell made me reach out, open my hand, take what hung from the branch and bring it to my mouth. My eyes played no part: the smell is what made me bring the fruit to my mouth. I felt its fresh, smooth skin with my lips, my tongue, and I sank my teeth into it.

(Stardust, stardust. I, too, am nothing more than stardust. But fertile dust, active, creating, generating, that's the very nature of that primordial dust.)

---

3. "*contra el bocado se estuvo / de Adán, sin probar bocado*" Sor Juana Inés de la Cruz, *Concepción, primero nocturno*, "Villancico I," *Obras completas*. Note that the quote is misused here, because the original villancico refers to the Virgin Mary, not Eve.

—

The cool flesh of the fruit—solid but fleeting, a study in opposites, airy but dense, light but heavy—delighted me when I bit it, not only its flavor and its smell, its crunchy, moist texture gave me unknown pleasure.

What was Eden like? In brief, not like it is here.

It was a confined, restricted space. Nature was absent. Eden was an abstract plaything, a place where time did not exist, no night, no seasons, no rain, no wind, no drought, no cold, no distance; it was one dimensional. The Sun did not beat down, there was no ice. If there had been water in Eden, it would never have boiled. There was no steam in Eden either.

It defied earthly logic. It was a kind of orchard in which everything was artificial, because though there were flowers and fruits, they weren't true flowers and fruits, they had no vitality, they didn't seek the Sun's light, they had no roots; there was no water, no air, no rocks, nothing that looked like earth on the ground.

Artists who have attempted to depict Eden have captured a little of what it was like, when, for example, they paint impractical and absurd things that defy all logic. Even if they don't look exactly like Eden, they are similar, in a way; distorting what Eden was, they only graze the surface, because it really was like a painting, a representation, but not on canvas or paper. Color, yes, it did have color, but without gradations, and not the four primary colors but all colors at once, without different tones or shades or combinations.

Adam also tried to recreate Eden, that's why he was so keen to domesticate animals. Because everything in Eden was orderly, as if planned out by a mind that was capable of thinking only on paper, in rigid shapes and plain colors.

In Eden I didn't know I was me, and I had no idea that Adam was right beside me. It goes without saying that we never dreamed, because we never slept, there was no sleeping, no waking; so the premise that Thunder took one of his ribs while he was sleeping to create me is a lie, from beginning to end. And it was also a lie to say that Adam grew crops and kept livestock. No. Eden was Eden, untouched by human hands.

Another fallacy is that in Eden living creatures and other things were given names.

"And the serpent, Eve?"

"Serpent? No, there was no serpent either! There was, however, the thing they call the 'apple,' and it was a fruit like the ones here on Earth."

"Is it true that in Eden Thunder spoke with the angels, and that they spoke with the Serpent?"

"No, I don't think so. Thunder didn't speak. It didn't communicate with language. It just rumbled things that weren't translatable into words . . . We didn't have words, we just nodded . . ."

"Were you in awe of Thunder?"

"We weren't capable of feeling awe. We kept our eyes on the heavens only because we didn't walk on all fours. Once in a while we cast our eyes down, just a reflex. We also couldn't look sideways (Adam and I never exchanged glances in Eden, I never saw the spark in his eyes)."

"You mean you didn't worship Thunder?"

"Of course not."

"Who started referring to Thunder as a deity—God, Divine, Eternal, the All-Powerful, the Creator, things like that?"

"Adam did, out of the blue, but he did so after we had come to know the power of Earth."

—

Eden was no orchard. The apple was the only fruit there with scent and flavor.

It's impossible to describe the creatures and the plants but let me try: They looked like they were made of lifeless matter, but that's not specific enough. They were completely untouched by the passage of time because they were in Eden.

All the creatures in Eden were devoid of earthly light, unable to experience touch, smell, taste, and sound. You could say they were "hollow," immaterial. I repeat: it wasn't as though they were made of paper, cloth, or paint, because all three of those have some kind of smell or flavor.

Nor was Eden made of light, like the angels, or darkness, like the ones called demons who are the inverse of light. It was neither one nor the other: Eden was like illuminated night.

Eden was not "attractive." It wasn't desirable, desire didn't exist there. Nor was it "appealing"; it neither attracted nor repelled. Nor was it plain. It was something else altogether, in a class of its own.

The one and only sweet-smelling, tasty apple hung from the branch of a tree, alone. Could it have been planted there—an intervention? If that were the case, who put it there? Was there a gardener in Eden? Even if that were the case, in Eden we didn't have imagination, so there was no way an Edenite could have imagined such a foreign object.

There is no apple without imagination, and there was no being with imagination in Eden. Who made the apple, then? Who? Or what?

Who in Eden had altered the cheerless, constant presence of Thunder? (Thunder, whom some refer to as male, thanks to Adam and his acolytes.) Or could it be that Thunder created it, betraying itself?

The apple was the key that set us free. It made us understand ourselves, making us who we were. Who had done this?

Some suppose it was the handwork of one of the angels but there's no evidence; as far as I know there were no angels in Eden, they stayed around the periphery.

There's no doubt that neither the angels nor the delicious fruit came from Eden, although the latter was certainly there.

"In the center, Eve? Was the apple at the heart of Eden?"

"That has nothing to do with it. Everything there was the center, or it didn't have a center at all. It's like saying that the surface of earth has a center. It doesn't. There wasn't one in Eden either."

I moved my hands toward the apple. I touched it. Its skin was a different temperature—unlike stone, unlike my body, unlike air; its texture felt completely foreign, a warning of the unknown—it wasn't smooth like lambskin or sharp like my teeth, it was neither water nor rock. Neither light nor darkness. Nor chaos.

The apple's skin awakened my own skin, giving me the courage to tell my hand, "Take it!"

In one swift motion I yanked the apple from the branch. I touched its skin to my lips. Once again it promised the unknown. I opened my mouth. My tongue touched it. I bit down. I chewed, it was sweet, and the tinkling bell sound the apple's flesh made when my jaws crushed it echoed in my ears. I chewed with gusto, my jaws yearning to bite the apple again to hear that pealing, that sweet thunder, that crushing sound.

Immediately, or simultaneously, I felt an enormous wave of pleasure, or perhaps it was a lightning bolt that started inside me and moved outward, lightning that didn't burn but was gentle—though that's not quite right, because I didn't tremble and it didn't hurt, although it was intense, caustic, a lashing of sheer pleasure, piercing, expanding through me.

The apple's flavor awakened my taste, my hearing, my smell,

my sight: my consciousness. Everything changed with that bite. And I mean it when I say "everything" because when I've said that before it has been taken as an indication of my lack of restraint, not the accuracy of my word choice.

I continued chewing the pulp that was in my mouth. Each bite was another sound, another flavor, another burst of pleasure.

Without thinking I offered it to the one next to me, the one I was just becoming aware of because my skin was awakening. I offered it to him and for the first time I looked at him with desire.

Before he even touched the apple, Adam looked me in the eyes (for the first time) and understood that something had changed. It was a schism; suddenly we were burdened with a life we didn't comprehend. That first look I gave him was a cascade. The way he looked at me . . . was denser, more stable, not fluid.

Adam took the apple, he felt it and he bit it, experiencing the same things I had—the pealing of its crunching flesh, its sweet flavor, the lashing, the lightning, the wound . . . I interlaced the fingers of his free hand in mine. I felt his skin with my skin for the first time. I saw Adam and, seeing him, I saw myself, too. I realized we were naked.

(The crushing sound of the apple's flesh in my mouth, its crunchy pealing . . . it was something I had never heard before—because I had never heard anything at all. The delicate, crunchy fruit awakened my hearing . . . I heard everything inside my body, because the mouthful was inside me, awakening me . . . and awakening the music of the stars, the sounds of the universe . . .)

3

Nakedness, the Look, the Voices of the Trees

We were naked, to each other. I let go of Adam's hand. I needed to cover myself, cover him, hide our nakedness from each other's eyes. I tried to cut some leaves from the tree where the apple had hung.

The tree resisted and spoke to me. Its words were the first to be heard in Eden. It said:

"You have disobeyed! I won't give you my leaves! You won't get anything from me!"

I pulled with all my might trying to tear the leaves away, ignoring it, but they wouldn't budge. It repeated its words again and again and I *understood it* after many repetitions:

"You have disobeyed! I won't give you my leaves! You won't get anything from me!"

I tried to take some leaves from a nearby tree. It had the same reaction and it also spoke to me:

"You have disobeyed! You are made of flesh and now you will be condemned to the flesh! You shall be your own night!"

It repeated itself over and over again, until I understood "disobeyed." Whom or what had I disobeyed?

Adam, who was aware of our nakedness, hid among some plants with very small leaves.

Free from his gaze and from the sight of him, I looked slowly and carefully at the leaves on the trees around me, examining them. The pleasure the delicious fruit had created had awoken my curiosity and my ability to tell the difference between things.

I turned to a fourth tree that stood apart from the others. It was a giant, odorless fig tree. Its lowest leaves, which I could reach with my hands, were drooping but not dry, hanging from withered branches. They were fleshy and fibrous. And the tree didn't have a voice, as if its soul were elsewhere. Since it was withered, I pulled off a branch with three large leaves. It wasn't difficult, the branches cooperated, and the leaves still had some life in them.

Two of the leaves, like the other green ones on the tree, were as big as me; a third one was a little smaller. I separated the leaves from the branch and tore them with my hands and teeth, using their veins as strings to hang the pieces of the leaves from my neck and waist.

The fleshy leaves (thick and still somewhat pliant) covered the front of my body, leaving my back bare, but that didn't bother me, because it wasn't modesty I felt (as has been written), rather it was the knowledge that someone could see me *because I could see.*

Dressed in my apron of two leaves, I fitted Adam with a leaf skirt around his waist while he, bewildered and anguished by the sensations from the apple, seemed completely incapacitated. I tied another vein from the leaf around his neck to cover his chest, as I had mine.

When he felt my fingers touching his skin repeatedly, Adam reacted. He lowered his eyes, which were still shining from the pleasure the fruit had given him. He raised his gaze and without taking his eyes off me he motioned that he was going to pass the apple to me. I gave him a look to ask him to hold it until I was finished arranging the aprons hanging around our shoulders and waists and the little skirt made from the large, thick-veined, fibrous leaves of the silent fig tree.

The apple had awoken a practical instinct in me, too.

I touched what remained of the apple he was holding between two fingers; his hand was steady, but it wavered, almost imperceptibly. Adam let go of the bitten fruit, almost letting it fall into my palm. Again, I bit where its skin covered its flesh. The sensation was even more intense. I chewed. I must have had the same anguished expression I had seen on Adam's face. I didn't want to stop chewing it, I didn't want to keep chewing it, I wanted that mouthful to be everlasting, not to pass down my throat, but I couldn't keep it in my mouth because my entire body desired it eagerly, impatiently, desperately . . . it wanted that pleasure . . .

I let the second mouthful pass down my throat and brought the last piece of the apple to my mouth. When I bit into it, I felt that same many-pleasured wave or lightning bolt once more.

While I was biting the apple, Adam picked up two of the withered branches I had cut from the fig tree and tied what was left from the veins of the leaves to them. Adam's hands had also awoken.

4

Thunder

Thunder boomed, expressing its anger with a "Why? Why eat the only sipid apple in all insipid Eden?"

Haughty Thunder used its own language, if you can call it language, the same language that everything in Eden had in common. In Eden we shared Thunder's speech, though you couldn't really call it speech.

The only exception was that the trees that denied me their leaves spoke language with words and grammar, with Time. They spoke because I had bitten that delicious fruit, because in the beginning there was the apple. The logical thing would have been if the tree that gave me the fruit had spoken, but in Eden logic didn't exist (nor in the Universe, but that's another story).

The trees observed my lack of action. That's how the plant kingdom is: they perceive with sensitivity, they adapt immediately; they're the most intelligent beings of all—they understand without thinking, taking things in and acting accordingly.

Edenic language—or Thunder's—was part of every fruit, every growing thing, every animal—even we could copy it, if awkwardly; but as I explained, Thunder's (and our) language wasn't truly a language because there wasn't a trace of grammar—no verbs, no inflection. Thunder used it to make pronouncements, as if the sounds were made of stone, those sounds in which it was impossible to vary a single syllable because they were long aaahs or ooohs, understandable only by their frightening tone—sounds like those made by shovels and hatchets, like rumbling winches or frenzied hammers, nothing that would come out of a mouth; rather, they were like something made by a firearm or gunpowder, or something otherworldly, like lightning.

So, in this sound of things, Thunder boomed. It knew what had happened. It knew we had tasted the flavor of a fruit foreign to Eden, and it knew how we had reacted. It didn't ask us, and we didn't try to hide it or ourselves. But it didn't utter curses either. How could it when Thunder couldn't speak? The part about the curse was added by those who came to hate me because I'm the one they came from, the one who caused the human condition, because I gave birth to all womankind with my own body. Adam never had that ability, one I gained through my own determination. Because when we left Eden, I wasn't capable of childbearing.

5

Thunder Butchers the Animals, Their Hides

While I still had that last bite of the apple in my mouth, Thunder murdered a number of beasts in Eden. I say "butchered" but it wasn't quite like that because in Eden, as I said, Time exercised no power. Things happened for the slightest reason, without them actually happening, because action requires the presence of Time.

(Only Adam and I were subject to Time, and only after partaking of the forbidden fruit.)

When Thunder killed those strange beasts, which, until that moment, seemed to have no hearts, muscles, bones, or skin, Eden was bathed in blood. I couldn't breathe. The final exhalations of those beasts filled the air with suffocation. The final breath, the lethal air that Thunder had blown into the cavities surrounded by their lips, or whatever you call those things around their beastly mouths, stank.

I breathed, drowning in their blood, in their death-breath.

The beasts, flayed without any visible tools, and their hides, instantly tanned, became our coats, cut and sewn with neither scissors nor thread. Like two large bags or sacks, they covered our fig leaves. Heavy yet pliable, like a second layer of human skin, they were perfect for protecting our naked bodies, covering us without dressing us; it was the work of Thunder, that hand unaffected by Time, impervious to action and to touch. An Edenic hand that made things happen without lifting a finger, without buttons or needles.

By biting the apple and tearing the dried leaves of the fig tree, I introduced Time into Eden, but Eden was oblivious to this introduction and remained essentially unchanged. Thunder's desires had their own particular logic; my actions and desires became subject to the laws of time.

Adam also changed, he had taken a bite (like me), he was marked by the loss of comprehending or expressing himself in Thunder's rumbling language (as I was).

Adam held a branch of the fig tree in each hand.

6

Eden Stank

Eden ejected us, it stank of dead animals; the only thing to do was leave.

But how to leave? I looked around me. I saw an aperture, a door, something that the bite of the apple had opened.

I went back to the tree where I had taken the delicious fruit.

I scrutinized it again: there were no other fruits, but at its base shone a single seed: black, elongated, with a fine point at one end and rounded at the other. It looked a little bit like the seed of a mamey, but it was smaller and rough to the touch. That's why mamey is sometimes called the original fruit or the fruit of Paradise, which couldn't be more wrong.

I picked up the seed. I put it under my armpit. The pleasure the fruit had awakened in me had made me covetous.

I returned to Adam, who was holding the two branches like staffs.

We stopped at the newly formed threshold of Eden, that opening where cold was entering. We both closed our coats, keeping our arms and hands inside them, including Adam's staffs. The ample hides wrapped around us.

It only took one step to leave the sinister, lethal command of Thunder behind, to leave so-called Eden.

END OF BOOK ONE

Loose papers which were interspersed among the pages of the first book

A PAPER OF EVE'S:
There are some who deny Chaos existed. That in the beginning there was a sea of (primordial) fresh water called Abzu, and a sea of salt water, called Tiamat, and that they begat a being in constant connection with the clouds; that was mist, Mummu. There was nothing but the two bodies of water; no sky, no land, not even a patch of ruddy swamp. These two bodies of water were the beginning of everything.

ANOTHER PAPER OF EVE'S:
It's said that man is defined as a being who eats. But what is eaten is also defined by who eats it: the unbitten apple that hung from the branch of the fruit tree would otherwise have rotted. I gave it meaning because I enjoyed it, and I gave us meaning, too: feelings, intuition, action, desire, pleasure—the word I was able to hear it say to the trees.

ANOTHER PAPER, ANOTHER VOICE:
It was the apple's fault, not Eve's. She responded reasonably to temptation: apples are for eating, they're delicious. If they had said to her "Jump into this abyss," Eve would not have jumped. If they had asked her to kiss a snake, she wouldn't have done that either. The apple was another story.

What would have become of us if Eve hadn't bitten the apple? Man did not come from earth: he came from fruit, the fruit bitten by a woman. And not just any old fruit: it was called "forbidden." With her fiery disobedience she broke the orb that was not to be eaten. Eve invented the basis of cooking.

The unbitten apple would only have rotted. But between Eve's teeth, it became a delicacy, its flavor eliminated the passage of time. That bite was eternity in an instant.

With that bite, Eve gave us culture; we owe the foundations of Mankind to her. She gave us the knowledge of our nakedness, the desire to clothe ourselves, to leave Paradise, to work for our bread, or land itself. And all by responding to that call to bite a beautiful apple, which was delicious.

Eating food, which was the result of this transgression, was the beginning of everything, the beginning of History.

The eternity of savoring that bite of the apple could never be repeated. Eve thought, "Ah! If only one could eat all the time!" Since it was impossible to keep that bite in her mouth, since the savoring of it would inevitably end, her tongue began to move restlessly, and her lips, skin, head, and hands, too; they were missing something. And so the Word was born—from pleasure, the end of pleasure, pain, cold, taste. Human words would not exist without that apple being bitten by Eve. Before that they spoke only God's language, which has become incomprehensible to us.

ANOTHER PAPER OF EVE'S:
Because I was aware of my hands, I was able to make our first clothes from the dry leaves of the fig tree, tearing them crudely so we could wear them as aprons and skirts. My hands felt and perceived, they imagined and danced, they moved as they had never moved before, there in Eden. Because the pleasure the apple filled me with had made me aware of my hands; after Eden

45

they were able to become the hands of an artisan, despite the fact I was not born of man. If it weren't for my intervention, we'd be naked bipeds; we would never have known our nakedness, never have talked, never had language; we'd just make rumbling sounds.

ANOTHER:
Some maintain that, without the bite of the apple that deprived us of our inheritance, Nature would have continued its course, as was the case with the sky, fish, animals, plants, rocks, sand, and the virgin Earth; and that war, violence, terror, plundering and pillaging and destruction would not have reigned. But that's a huge lie that doesn't account for the violence of the tiger, the voracity of the spider, the desire of the wind. We are contained by our own souls. Without that, woe betide the Earth! It would be the cradle of vermin, begetting ever-more monstrous vermin, lakes would be filled with blood, and perpetuate a species that would be unaware all was death, death, death.

"It's a mistake, Eve, to say such a thing. Humankind is the very ruin and destruction of the Earth. We're the greatest consumer of vermin, destroyers, bathing the land and the lakes in something much more sordid than sordidness, poisoning the pretty fish, the birds . . ."

"That's enough, Scila, we know what you think."

"And it's not true. You're younger so you don't know how depressing the fields were before we women . . ."

"It was Cain, wasn't it? He's the one who began . . ."

ANOTHER:
Eve says she didn't have a mother, but that's not right: her mother was the apple.

We're descended from fruits, which in turn descend from

46

the trees, which in turn are descended from the seeds inside the fruits: a complete circle of life.

The bit about being made of clay and the breath of some other being is a malicious lie invented by beings enamored with death. Who on Earth would think that we're related to pottery? No one! Not even some of the drunkards I know! To become what we are we must pass through our mother's sap, not the fire and the kiln!

ANOTHER:

We were different in Eden. Though we inhabited our bodies, we were far from being what we are now. Maybe at the moment of taking the apple we ceased slithering because the serpent explained with gestures that, before tempting us, it walked upright, and that we had slithered along the ground like it did now. But it wasn't the serpent's gestures that got me to try the fruit; it was the scent of the apple.

We left Paradise by mouth, then, the mouth that had bitten the apple. And we went by mouth to Earth. The rest of our bodies like empty tree trunks, made of flesh.

Because with my mouth, with that bite, I pronounced our first word, and it rang out. Because when the word was born, memory was born and that's why I remember: it was more than a mere syllable, it sounded more like a moan of pleasure or pain. But to moan like that we needed to be able to inhabit the empty trunks of our bodies, newly erect and strange to us, as if we had just found them.

ANOTHER:

"Well, I'm no daughter of God's and I'm no daughter of Man either; I'm the daughter of the fruit of a tree who responded to imagination."

47

ANOTHER (which we'll leave in this transcription because it's illegible to us):
"She couldn't have had the faintest idea of what 'before' was like (the 'before me' that Eve speaks about)."

"The apple marked the beginning of perception. Before it, the senses didn't exist."

"Earth followed its route around the Sun dozens of times before Eve reconstructed what had happened before and called it "the past." She did that to make sense of time, to give it shape, with an aesthetic sensibility; she wasn't attempting to tell a story that was true to the facts. Which is why it's so engaging; it illuminates part of her life, which is ours, too, because she is The Mother of All."

BOOK TWO

7

The Hooves and the Memory of Eden

We looked somewhat like animals because of the stinking hides Thunder had wrapped us in and the hooves we had for feet. Yes, we had hooves. Our hooves were the same as those of the horses and goats that aided us on the steep, rugged slopes of the Divine Mount. Memory keeps us ever aware of four hooves—two for the male, two for the female (me)—all identical. Not "female" hooves or "male" hooves, but genderless, just like us.

Could it be that Thunder gave us our hooves at the same time as the hides, to make us more like animals?

Or could it be that we became aware of our nakedness because, before biting the apple, we were covered with some kind of special skin, which disappeared with the first bite? That we were covered with it when we lived there, and that's why I couldn't hear, feel, see, or perceive anything? Were our hooves what remained of that skin?

Could it be that we had been one person with four legs, a single being with a woman's face looking in one direction and a man's facing the other, both bodies covered in a shared skin, joined at the spine?

Before the apple, in Eden, I had no consciousness. I knew about my body because of the apple. Did that epidermis that covered our bodies fall off when I bit the apple, and was that why I became aware of my nakedness, aware of our torsos, heads, legs?

Was it Thunder who had covered us in that epidermis, if there had been one, replacing it with the hides when it disappeared?

We looked a bit like fauns. The hooves protected our feet. And though they gripped the ground well, when we were enveloped in the animal skins that Thunder covered us with, we stumbled.

The desire to leave Eden propelled us to take our first steps as though someone had pushed us from behind; because of the steep pitch of the slope, its slippery surface, and the unfamiliar weight of our bodies, we fell.

Hobbled by the sacks of hide Thunder had wrapped us in, our hands confined within them, we stood stiff and tall but with a poor sense of balance.

8

The Sight of Earth

Being in Eden was like being nowhere; without time there is no space.

When we crossed the threshold, we were at the peak of the Divine Mount.

The immensity of Earth spread at our feet.

The view was sublime.

Our eyes *perceived*: the Sun began to disappear on the horizon (to hide itself, as if it, too, had felt naked for the first time), the sky was tinged with vibrant colors, the skin of the globe came alive in different colors: greens, grays, blues, magentas, violets, golds . . . The seas, the rivers, the mountains, everything on Earth glowed.

If I had been at all prepared for this sight, perhaps I would have thought, "Now this is a universe; it's not drenched in blood from skinning animals and Thunder doesn't rumble down from on high."

We fell and were reminded of Eden by the stink of the stiff, heavy skins and the rough, sticky patches of dried blood on them, which caked onto our skin. Eden's insipid blandness had been altered by Thunder's crime against the animals, which literally stuck to us much, to our chagrin. The comparison between Eden and Earth became inevitable: we had arrived in Paradise.

Invisible in the distance, the movement of the giants and other creatures could be felt because everything on Earth—the fish, insects, birds, quadrupeds, and reptiles—was gathered in a celebration of life. O, lovely Earth! Our world!

We slipped on the black sand on the steep slope at the summit of the Divine Mount. Behind me Adam stumbled and fell, hitting the ground again and again, like me.

We looked up and fell, fell and looked up. Alas! This was how human perception first developed. We learned with each clumsy fall, sharpening our senses.

A ridge stopped our fall. Resting on flat ground, we breathed deep, we were completely winded. When our breathing had slowed, we took two or three long breaths and took another step to continue our descent. Moving almost in unison, we fell again, not because of the steepness of the Divine Mount but because of our weakness, as strong a force as gravity itself. So, we paused our journey, which was a gift.

9

The First Ridge

I have not laid eyes on such a place ever since. We had landed on a narrow stretch of land between two breathtaking, loudly bubbling lakes on a ridge that looked like it had been designed impulsively by a steady hand, with no trace of the undulations or irregularities so commonplace on Earth.

One of the two lakes was red, tinged by the color of the fiery sky, the other was dark lava; both boiled away.

We had fallen on the stretch of black sand between the two lakes; it was four steps wide and, like the lakes, was about three or four times that long.

At the edge of the ridge, on the banks of the two lakes, the World awaited, illuminated by the mocking, amber-colored light of the setting Sun.

The two lakes roared nonstop, two living monsters; their waters made waves, eddies, whirlpools, and waterspouts. The distinct borders of the lakes looked unlikely to contain them.

Today the oceans continue to behave in this same manner: stubborn, forceful, just like those bodies of liquid I saw on that ridge.

I saw fear in Adam's eyes. Fear of the two threatening, fiery pools of liquid that flanked the narrow piece of ground we were resting on; fear of the wide, glittering World at our feet; and fear of the vibrantly colored sky. He grasped my arm firmly; the two thick hides we were wearing still separated us, but I could feel him holding on to me nervously.

Adam turned around. I didn't resist; I was curious to see what the place we had just left behind was like, because we had been in such a hurry that I had seen only the coarse black sand that had slid down the slope with us.

10

The Guardian Angel and Fire

When he saw Eden, Adam wanted to go back. He took a step. I
stopped him and pointed at the black peak with nearly vertical
slopes we had just slid down. At its zenith, an unspeakably beautiful being made of bright, white dust floated midair, shimmering
with luminous, refracted light, guarding the entrance to Eden. Its
shape was similar to ours. It held a live flame in its hand. Its scent
was complex and exquisite, too.

When it saw me looking, it waved its arm, its fire.

Led by Adam, we approached the steep slopes of black sand that
led to the entrance to Eden. Adam wanted to scale that sandy
peak and return to the land of Thunder—an absurd idea, because
unless we could fly it would have been impossible to scale that
rough, nearly vertical peak we had just descended, slipping and
falling; there was nothing to grasp on to to scale its heights. I
let myself be guided by this frightened man because I wanted to
touch the Angel.

But then Adam noticed the guardian Angel. The sight hit
him hard, a groan escaped from his mouth. It wasn't so much
the sound of the fear in his eyes or in his hand grabbing my arm.
There was awe in his groan, and for good reason; the brilliance of
the Angel's body was breathtakingly beautiful.

Adam tried to take a step back, but I pulled him forward; I
wanted to touch the Angel, to feel its body of light.

Angel, apple: temptation.

I moved decisively; I had no intention of returning to Eden. The view of the World that spread out behind me was marvelous. I wanted to be on Earth. But the beauty and bravado of the Angel captivated me.

The divine creature reacted to my approach by waving the fire more quickly. It didn't frighten me. Adam tried to hold me back. I let go of his hand and moved closer to the Angel. It descended toward me, becoming more threatening and more beautiful. It burned as brightly as the fire it waved in its hand.

When I felt attracted to the apple in Eden I had not known of its crunchy freshness. The Angel did show me its cards: it was made of fire, which made it irresistible.

I opened the heavy coat of hide that Thunder had wrapped around us, intending to bare my chest and feel the Angel, so I lifted the apron of fleshy fig leaves that had started to dry out. I left my chest bare and felt the beauty of the Angel with my own skin, wanting it even more. Obviously, I couldn't reach out and grab the Angel, bring it to my mouth and bite it, as I had the apple. I just wanted to touch it. Behind me, Adam shouted, trying to imitate Thunder's rumble, attempting to warn me of the danger.

I could feel that the sight of my naked body made the Angel feel the same stirrings I was feeling. It brandished its fire, waving ever more vigorously, making it burn more brightly as it moved toward me. My leaf-apron, which I was holding at arm's length to bare my chest, caught fire, burning up and burning me. The fire ate up the flesh of the leaves and slowed at the veins (a careful observer would say that the fire ran along their spines, the leaves showering sparks).

I pulled the flaming apron off my neck, holding it out from my body, but I didn't drop it.

I tore the rest of the leaves from my body, and wrapped them around the burning ones, trying not to extinguish their flames, to leave them burning.

So, with one hand holding those fiery contents (like the Angel, in my own way), I turned around and stepped toward Adam. He took a step back. I didn't see the look on his face, I didn't understand what he was doing. I was afraid he would take another step back and fall into the boiling liquid in the lake.

I locked eyes with Adam to warn him, and I saw that he was able to understand that I wasn't another angel, that I was *speaking* to him about the twin threat of the two burning lakes. He paused. He even understood that there was no chance of return since the guardian Angel was preventing us from attempting the ascent (which in itself was impossible).

I turned to look at the Angel again. It threw a stone (larger than my head) at me; the stone grazed my arm and crashed behind me, between my feet and Adam's. The impact broke it in half. Inside it was hollow, filled with blue-gold crystals whose little pyramids were like a poor imitation of the Angel's brilliance.

The fright of the stone nearly hitting me and the heat of the leaves burning made me drop them. As if they were endowed with their own wisdom, they floated down, dancing, sinuous and elegant, landing on the crystals of the Angel's stone, the lovely weapon that the beautiful Angel had thrown at me, splitting it in half so it could catch the embers in a cradle of crystals.

I fit together the two halves of the stone, filled with the patient, slow-burning thick leaves. The two halves didn't fit perfectly; the edges had chipped upon impact.

I laid that stone (with its soul of crystal teeth and fiery heart) in a fold of the animal hide Thunder had dressed me in and wrapped myself in that beastly coat once more.

Adam and I gazed at each other. When our eyes met, we reached an agreement: we would continue on our way.

But the Angel's stone with the fire inside was burning my chest. I saw a piece of smooth, black slate at our feet. I picked it up (it was freezing), opened my hide coat, and placed it between my chest and the stone. A half-step away I found another piece of the dark slate; I put it between my arms and the stone.

The mute fig tree (with its odorless, tasteless Edenic fruit) never imagined the role it would play: accomplice to the theft of fire. I wasn't in fire's destiny, but I took it and made it mine, my creation.

Adam and I descended a short way, with greater difficulty in my case because it was not easy to carry my burden, keeping in place the two slates protecting me from the geode.

I stopped, and I stopped Adam. I gestured for him to hand me the fig leaves he was wearing as an apron and skirt; he pulled them from his neck and his waist and gave them to me. Quickly, I separated their supple veins with my teeth; I opened the two halves of the stone and added the flesh of his leaves to my burning ones, put the stone back together and tied it with the veins.

I embraced my cargo, made from the two pieces of slate and the broken stone filled with crystals and burning leaves, wrapped in the veins of Adam's fig leaves.

I wrapped myself in the hide more tightly. Adam did the same with his coat.

Adam was in a hurry to put some distance between us and the Angel, so he forged ahead hardly noticing whether or not I was following him. Once again, he was acting out of fear and fear had blinded him because the Angel had already disappeared; there was no need to run away, but Adam hadn't even noticed.

Staring at the ground, he avoided looking at the Earth's immensity or the sky, which had lit up like it was on fire.

We jumped to the next ledge.

11

The Second Ridge. The Slope.
The Cold and the Weeping

The second ridge was covered in white snow. The change in temperature was extreme; the heat from the boiling lakes on the ridge above us rose toward Eden, it did not radiate down the mountain.

We traversed it nervously (as if we feared that traps lay below the layer of white snow) and continued our descent. We hurried along, aided by gravity and the slipperiness of the ice. We slid along like we were skating whenever we weren't held back by the unevenness of the slope. We ran when we could.

Adam removed from his coat the two branches of the fruit tree he had taken in Eden, leaning on them for balance, so I fell behind.

He waited for me far below where there was no more snow; soft, grayish ash cushioned the ground. The cold had intensified.

We continued along clumsily, taking large strides, falling often. The terrain was uneven, and it was hard to gauge because the sky was becoming a darker blue in places, indicating that night was advancing. We ran more and we fell more, until the slope became less steep. Then we could slow our momentum, the inertia of the descent, and take a rest.

The hides that covered us were completely stiff. Despite the intense cold they stank, and made us stink, too. They had become fragile as they hardened, and we had torn them when we fell. The blood they had covered us with when we donned them was no longer sticky; it was like a rough varnish, strange and uneven and pungent, too. While we were resting, a blast of freezing wind stripped some clouds from the sky and we were embraced in a new, silvery light, an auric light, the light of the Moon.

We continued down the slope, falling repeatedly.

The full Moon shone above us.

I cried tears of cold. It was a physical reaction, not an expression of grief. It would be some time before crying evolved into another way of communicating, of expressing what is difficult to put into words. Back then it just expressed grief in the language of things.

Without those first tears of my semi-being, crying as we know it today would not exist. Those tears bonded me to all things without language and without life.

Nothing else is like crying. When I bit the apple, we became what we are; when I cried those tears of cold, feeling became part of our nature.

On our journey we didn't raise our eyes from the ground, we had become fearful creatures. Adam's fear was contagious, and I caught it. Although the Adamic and the Eveic have always been separate, his fear infected me during this phase of our fall.

This contagion didn't unite us. Adam and I always had one simple and absolute difference: each of us is different from the other because of that bite I took. And among all Eve's descendants there are no two exactly alike. None, not even monozygous twins.

But there's also no doubt that, tied to each other as we are, we sometimes reflect the other. There, on that journey, I mirrored Adam's fear for a time.

12

The Moon (Absent and Present). Laughter

The Moon's bright light accompanied us on that stretch of our descent.

After the full Moon the Sun slowly reappeared. And we kept on running. After the Sun, the Moon returned in its brilliance, silvering the grass and the leaves on the trees.

We ran without stopping, not pausing to notice and feel our surroundings, except when we fell into short bursts of catatonic sleep, taking turns—Adam and I never slept at the same time; we slept on our feet, sleeping profoundly for a few seconds at a time while the other stopped to evaluate our surroundings, vigilant, and then we'd start running again, hardly taking a breath.

Hurrying, we walked in silver moonlight and harsh sunlight until, one night, we were enveloped in total darkness. We had to stop.

The sky had eaten the Moon. Night was everything, everywhere. Total night, unfamiliar to us. It was nothing like eternal midday in Eden.

Our fear turned to terror. We didn't know how to form the question that had settled silently in our bones: would we be left without light forever? Would we live wrapped in darkness? Because of this new fear I moved closer to Adam. I felt him shaking.

His shaking snapped me out of my fear of doing anything. I took the bundle with the angel-stone out of my capacious, animal-hide coat. I squatted to place it on the ground. I untied it and opened the two halves of that angel-stone. The sparks jumped, illuminating the thick and thin stalks of twisting grass in our dried-out surroundings. The grasses were tough but dry, so I tried to tear them, and it worked. I put them with the embers from the fig leaves, blew on them and they burned, creating more sparks.

Adam broke his dried branches from Eden into pieces, squatted down next to me, and moved a few pieces toward the sparks. We both began to blow, bringing the embers to life, and we had a fire: fat orange flames.

We breathed deeply. We had been running and running without resting, without thinking, who knows how long. We looked at one another, squatting awkwardly, dressed in our coats, those animal-hide sacks. The fire crackled. Time changed its beat.

Adam got up and gathered some dry leaves, stacking them with more broken, dry twigs. Using the slates, I moved the burning ones on top of the pile Adam had made. The fire grew and grew again when we fed it another piece of the Edenic branches Adam had been carrying, creating those unusually fat orange flames once more.

We squatted down again next to the fire we had not stolen from the gods—the Angel had come to me of its own accord.

The fire created a short-lived midday. It extinguished our fear of the night we thought was eternal. Playing with the flames we felt united. We kept on playing and Adam's coat nearly caught fire; I half burned a finger trying to save it and our attempts were so clumsy (it sufficed to keep flammable things out of the flames) that we laughed for the first time.

Laughing for the first time: this, along with the apple and the tears, was shaping us, giving us spirit. The apple, shape. Laughter, spirit. Tears, both together.

(Taste, pleasure, apple. Cold, journey, tears. What made

laughter? What power did that extraordinary feeling endow us with, the same feeling that allows us to appreciate beauty? Was it a delayed response to the experience of language with the trees in Eden?)

Because I had been so overwhelmed, I had not paid attention to the damage around the skin on my torso and hands from handling the fire-filled rock, not even the small and medium-sized burns on my finger.

But I did take time to find the seed of the only fruit with flavor in Eden; it had stuck to the sweaty hair under my arms. I touched it and put it back in the same hidden place on my body.

13

Night

Night arrived, accompanied by a symphony of sounds; since we didn't recognize the noises, they all blended together. The crackling of the fire made them seem louder, and more confusing.

Eden was a mute, silent place apart from Thunder's rumbles and interjections. The first thing I ever heard apart from Thunder's croaking was the crunchy apple; the second thing was the words the trees spoke; the third was the bubbling of the two burning lakes, which I didn't hear when we passed them the second time because I was concentrating so hard on the fire. Without a question, these sounds made those experiences more memorable. But it wasn't until that completely dark night, the one we spent by the fire, that I understood we were in a world of sounds, surrounded by noises. Language was born with (and from) the trees; the music of the World was born between the two lakes, because that was the first time we heard Earth's song, and it was during that first night, in the darkness, that we witnessed it for ourselves: music was part of our new life. Although we didn't fully understand that because we didn't have words yet.

I won't describe our fear and terror again; my perception wasn't limited to the physical: cold, fear, or the wonder and pleasure of fire. We realized that on Earth we were in Time, alive, vulnerable—as the pain from my burns and the bruises from my falls reminded me. We were no longer immortal inhabitants of a place where everything was uncorrupted, divine, obedient, lacking volition—nothing good, nothing bad, no clothes, no scent, no taste, no words—silent and unashamed, fleshless.

The crackling fire comforted us and made us feel safe. We lay down; we fell asleep.

14

Eve Dreams

And then the most extraordinary thing of that whole night happened: I dreamed. I knew I was dreaming. I'll tell you about the last dream now (the one I remember because the others disappeared like clouds without tails to grab on to):

I'm naked on a plain (which I hadn't seen in waking life, but which looked lovely in my dream). The Angel (bright, white dust) is behind me, objecting to my theft of the fire, wanting to punish me. I don't argue, I know the accusation is unfair, I didn't steal anything from him; fire can't be stolen, it's not limited in quantity.

I begin to run, and he follows me with his sword in one hand and the apple in his other. I can see him as if he's ahead of me, even though he's running behind me. He threatens me with the blade of his weapon, but I'm not frightened, I want the apple. He waves his sword; it bursts into flames. The fire distracts him. I surprise him and snatch the apple. The Angel seems to harden, as if he has turned to stone. I move the apple closer to the fiery sword. He trembles at my audacity, but he doesn't step back. I don't either, despite the intense heat on my hand. The Angel stands stock-still, the fire jumping and flickering in his immobile hand. I pick up a stick from the ground and drive it into the apple, moving it even closer to the fiery sword with the stick. I hold the apple in the flames, it gives off a scent unlike any other, the pleasant aroma of roasted apple. I hold it there even longer; my face is burning. The apple changes color. When it begins to smell like burning apple skin, I take it out. I turn around. I move away from the frozen Angel.

The scent of the apple, seasoned by the soft, intense aroma from the blackened skin, is everywhere. It's so strong that it dims the Angel's brightness.

I awaken.

It's still night, but the sky is blue. The world doesn't smell like golden roasted apple. Adam sleeps beside me, wrapped in his coat.

15

Eve and Adam

It was just the two of us alone in the wide world, without anyone to take care of us, protect us, watch over us, but we had fire on our side. Lying there, defenseless, the fire protected us from the beasts. The embers of the leaves and branches of the fig tree, which had grown its thick, timeless foliage in Eden, endured and shone.

I got up and squatted before the fire. I blew on the embers, adding another fistful of dry grass; the flames jumped. I stood up and took two steps, the fire at my back. The darkness was immense, as was the sky. I went over to Adam. I removed the rough coat the Creator had made for me; with swiftness and agility I got inside the coat enveloping Adam like a bag. I carefully closed it around us. We were naked and shielded from the cold, wrapped in the same animal hide.

16

Adam's Skin

I felt Adam's skin, soft like that of a child who never ages. I moved my tongue across his skin. It didn't taste the same as the apple, but there was something about it. I playfully bit his shoulder, waking him. In that one act I was calling him "man" and "companion."

It was the middle of the night. We were both awake. The birds began to chirp, as if they knew. They were welcoming us to the World with their persistent, repetitive song. Their sound—another kind of music—was a new lesson in language. They seemed to be speaking of something that was intimately connected to the tableau Adam and I presented, naked and bewildered inside one coat of stinking hide.

Adam gripped me in both arms in a way that was both frightening and fearless. It wasn't at all pleasant. I looked up and copied, as best I could, one of the birds' songs. Between the huge leaves of a bush the sky appeared purple, like a wound. I tried imitating another bird's coo-coo-ooo. I saw a point of light streak across the sky—perhaps a shooting star—which was turning blue. Adam let me go, slipping out of the hide we had been sharing and wrapped himself in mine, which was lying nearby. Thus covered, he squatted in front of the fire, stirring the coals and stoking it. I kept silent. I closed my eyes. I fell back asleep, without dreams, though I think only briefly.

17

Thirst

I awoke. We were thirsty, an irritating sensation; in Eden we had known neither thirst nor hunger. Fate had led us to pass the night three short steps from a spring that bubbled forth through a hole in some rocks on a nearly vertical part of the slope. We had never touched water but biting the apple had awoken our instincts. We both put our faces into the stream of water at the same time. The water was freezing. I reacted by pulling away. Adam didn't; he was the first to drink. And he drank again, his expression one of sheer pleasure. Overcoming my aversion to the coldness, I followed his example; immediately my thirst was relieved.

We rested on an outcropping next to the spring's source. Everything around us made sound: the leaves moving in the breeze, the footsteps of the animals, the bubbling of the spring, the soft wind. For the first time I saw a spider in its web, I watched a worm inch along, and there were other insects whose names I don't know, because there are no insects in Eden. Adam had another drink. He said, "water." And this was the first word we used to speak of drinking, springs, thirst.

Water. I still drink *water*, I still feel that combination of need and urgency, and the gift—its inherent luxury, the contrasting sensations: the painful cold, the satiation of thirst.

On the ground next to the spring there was a little puddle. I leaned over and saw my reflection; at first, I was frightened but only until I caught sight of Adam's reflection, too.

I touched my face, and it immediately became disfigured. I looked at myself for some time. Adam didn't seem interested; he turned away from the spring and lay down facing the Sun, blinded by its light.

I said the word *Eve* to name myself. Adam repeated it without turning to look at me. I named him, too, I called him *Adam* because I wanted to, Adam, my companion. He didn't repeat his name. The first name to be uttered twice was mine, Eve's, auguring its endurance.

18

Fire, the Protector

The fire kept the beasts at bay. We didn't allow it to die down whenever we weren't moving down the mountain. Bonfires, torches, precious embers: they were never far from us. I felt fire was a being like us, intuiting our fragility, our need for water, our dependence.

Without fire, sleeping would have been impossible; without sleeping we would have been unable to dream, not even while tossing and turning, not even in that state which creates a bridge between the universe of dreams and the one of waking. The bridge that creates a real, all-encompassing truth that has obvious influence on the state of waking: imagination.

But there was something else. The fire was a confirmation of the different elements: earth, water, air, fire.

And another thing: sleep.

19

Words

Both of us—Adam and Eve—treasured words; we repeated them and invented new ones. When we weren't busy doing something else, we played with them, altering them.

We learned to want to stop working because we wanted to be with words. When we stopped working that's all we did. Words accompanied our thoughts, observations, fears, even our moments of surprise. Later on, we used them like tools, to name our needs.

In between our observations and use of words we began to create our own music, at first with dried gourds containing seeds, hollow logs, little stones that made a sharp sound when you rubbed them, and strips of fibrous plants.

We made a name for the way water bubbled up from the ground, as if the words were made in our bodies—carved, cut, and polished there, tanned and stitched together by what lay beneath our skin, revealing their clarity when they arrived on our lips. The air we breathed morphed into words inside us and took on auditory form when it came back out. We populated the Earth with words. The trees, the plants, and the animals lived alongside them, and some were altered by the effect the syllables had on them.

Days flew by in the company of words. Through them, we knew to watch the Moon's regular waxing and waning; that the darkness of night was neither random nor unending; that the Sun would disappear at a point in the distance and return, rising at dawn with a "good morning."

20

White Darkness

The wind blew. A storm of spores began to fall, so thick that it blocked out sunlight. A different kind of night fell upon us. It was white, completely white, preventing our eyes from seeing anything but that thick whiteness. It was like a living organism. And it was irritating when we breathed.

Each gust of wind brought more spores, blinding us. We could no longer see spiderwebs, leaves on the trees, the mountainside, or our own reflections. There was a white curtain of darkness between us and everything else, a bright darkness. Breathing in that white darkness, clearing our throats and coughing, we could no longer see each other, like blind white shadows . . .

The trees outside of Eden were speechless: their ability to speak had been supplanted by their persistence and determination to reproduce, their spores replacing words, tracing shapes as they fell, forming bodies and blocks, breaking apart suddenly and coming back together, the words of a multitude, shouted and screamed, blinding.

Covered in this white blanket, by this silent screaming of the trees, we removed our animal hide coats, naked but unable to see our nakedness. There was something pleasant about being anonymous and becoming part of it. Adam particularly enjoyed it.

I missed being able to see and speak. I busied my hands while my body slept in that white night, feeling like it was rusting. I picked up something I found—later I realized it was the bone of a vulture—and broke it. I sucked out all the marrow until it was hollow. I blew into it. It made a noise. I made a small incision in its side, and then another. I blew into it again: it made a sweet sound, high-pitched and wavering.

That was our first flute.

21

The Rain. Eve's Dance

The rain fell. Torrential, terrible, jubilant, resonant, magnanimous; rain that was unlike air, unlike water, unlike earth, a different kind of substance: quick, hurried, persistent, chatty, unpredictable. It followed me, hounding me; I wanted it, it left without notice.

The air cleared. The blinding whiteness that had plagued us washed away. We could see the world again.

The weather was perfect. The clearness of the air, the accompanying silence, being able to see the creatures flying all around me, these things lifted my spirits.

It was the first time I danced.

"The first time Eve danced was just because, because the wind blew softly, because the leaves on the trees rustled. The effect of the apple was a thing of the past (it's just a memory now that she's in her dotage, her vitality waning). And it came to pass that fire no longer mattered to her, nor the seed she stole from Eden, nor edible roots, nor stalking wolves and vultures, not even Adam. Although it's possible Eve began to dance because when she raised her sights to the sky, she saw flying creatures in all shapes and sizes, swinging in the heavens, descending stairways in the air with sudden leaps. Flies, wasps, butterflies, birds of different colors and shapes, they all flew with agility, falling without crashing, like the thick, burning leaves that Eve says came from the fig tree, when they caught fire and little bits of them rose into the air, aflame. She danced to the sound of the gourds with dried sees inside them, which she shook in her dancing hands."

"Eve used words like another form of percussion to accompany her dances. She kept repeating, 'The serpent is good: it takes care of water underground.' Speaking to the beat and without pause, she told the story of the apple."

Biting the apple, crying from cold, laughing, dancing: we were becoming what we are.

22

The Bee

Adam is sleeping one day in his animal-hide coat, when a little insect comes close, like a buzzing sigh, with three golden stripes on its body. I look at it, curious. It buzzes. Is it striped to show how unpredictable its flight is, since it zigs and zags wherever it goes? I follow it with my eyes. It goes straight to a small, pale flower on a bush. It drinks. Goes to the next. Returns to Adam, from whom it does not drink, though his scent seems to appeal. It flies around and around Adam, buzzing nonstop.

Adam awakens, sees it, and gives it a name: bee. I repeat: bee. Then others begin to appear. The bees came into our lives without revealing their value to us.

23

The Beast and Our Flight

We neglect the fire. A four-legged beast, enormous and terrifying, switching its long, fat tail. The earth trembles with each of its steps. It crushes everything it sets foot upon, the ground itself appears to be affected by its weight. We didn't have time to name it. I snatched the fire stone, grabbed a handful of embers, put them inside, and then we both began to run. In our haste to escape, we left our coats behind.

The beast roars and goes straight for the robes of animal hide we had brought from Eden, attracted by their smell (and maybe the bee, too?). It lifts the coats with its muzzle, holding them between its jaws, continuing to roar; its paws beat the ground, but it stays in the same place.

We fled from that place without seeing anything else. We had no idea it would be so difficult to find a new place to satiate our thirst.

The days ahead were anxious ones.

END OF BOOK TWO

Eve's Loose Papers

A PAPER:

We fled, but before I continue with my story, let me explain that I was drunk without drinking a drop. Who wouldn't have been, in my place? One poet described me as awestruck, another called me confused, others said bewitched or seduced, countless others spoke of my wickedness and perversion, of my deals with the dark forces that, as is believed today, gave shape to the ever-changing universe. (An ever-changing shape that we believe is eternal and infinite but is neither. The constantly expanding universe that fit inside one finger is a thing of the past. We watch it change, a tiny piece of it, and we are dwarfed by its immensity, believing that we are the ones who create and destroy, believing that we are History.)

Of all the things I have been called by the bards I like "awestruck" best, but it's not accurate: I was inebriated.

I think I was drunk off the scent of the fruit before I even opened my mouth. My memories of that first instant after my first bite are like a drunken haze. It was the first time a person had seen with their eyes, had noticed, perceived. The creatures around me were unseeing, empty shells, blind and dreamless. No one and nothing could see anything or feel a ray of light or movement, not gases, not matter, not even its creator, antimatter.

I was the first to see. And the first to think about why I was seeing—or to see why I was thinking. As I said everything on high remained on high and what was below was in its place, too, as well as everything in between. But I couldn't see this at first. I had to be able to see.

"Eve, you never said, 'I love them more than mine own eyes.' Never."

ANOTHER PAPER OF EVE'S:

Whence and whither, how and with what were the leaves of the fig sewn? Were leaves sewn to leaves? Were they sewn to Eve's lips and then to Adam's? From the sky to their bodies? The version we know doesn't specify.

"They sewed fig leaves."

I have sewn fig leaves. Fig leaves have I sewn. I will sew fig leaves with fig tree, with my body and with Adam's, with the sky, and even with dark matter; I shall sew with anything and everything, because sewing is embroidering, giving meaning, understanding, interpreting, infusing, matching . . .

ANOTHER:

My full name is Eve Hawa. Was I called woman, and did I respond to that form of address? Don't bother asking; the wise answer would be, "Not that I recall." The foolhardy one would be: "In the beginning there was Eve."

ANOTHER:

We were never lifeless dust.

ANOTHER:

Adam stretched out on the ground and put his head in my lap. This gesture reminded me of the apple. The memory of the crunchy fruit made my tongue prickle and my palate, too. I said my first word, stimulated by the memory and inspired by the words the tree spoke. I spoke one syllable to Adam that meant *night*. Adam repeated: "night." He lifted his head. He looked me in the eyes. In the light of the flames from our small file I saw something I hadn't seen before, and I knew, even though I still didn't know how to say it, that I loved, and that this, coupled with my fatigue, my feelings, all the new things I was experiencing, including the novel passage of Time, had worn us out. We fell asleep

(I think:

that I believe in love,

I am a fish-creature,

directionless,

I am a brave animal,

but my body is bared,

surrendered to love,

for a moment I am,

or think I am,

what I hear).

ANOTHER (A SLIGHTLY DIFFERENT VERSION OF A PREVIOUS PASSAGE):
Thunder expressed itself like falling rock, without words, without verbs, without adjectives; like long oooohs and aaaahs emanating from a fearsome throat, like the blows of an axe or shovel or hammer; but not guttural like the sounds a mouth makes; more like a weapon, or gunpowder.

ANOTHER:
"You told us, Eve, that after the fall your mouth was empty but your ears were open and you heard voices, or something you later identified as voices or bells, something like music. That you thought it was coming from the Angel, the guardian of Eden. That you thought that his wings made a metallic noise, like a clapper striking a bell that exhaled a sound akin to the quiet laughter

of myriad voices, a conversation heard from such a distance that you can't be sure what language it is. It was a rhythmic, harmonious sound that was beautiful, endlessly beautiful.

"Of course, you also told us that 'when I ran, I heard nothing but the sound of the wind in my ears,' because in Eden we weren't surrounded by air but rather by a tepid emptiness, a void."

ANOTHER (FROM ONE OF EVE'S OTHER DAUGHTERS): The trees shed an enormous quantity of male and female spores so that some of them would find a mate and be fertilized. They needed this excess to ensure their reproduction. It turned daytime into white night.

Eve couldn't stand the white nights that lasted all day and all night, and that made breathing so difficult; she hated that blanket, the curtain, which the trees and plants drew across the land, far and wide.

That's why the first thing Eve begat was a huge, clumsy, ill-behaved, charmless thing, with a little tube for a nose, all wings. It was a proto-insect, heavy but able to fly. After many more attempts Eve succeeded in creating the creature that would make the air clear, pulling back the white curtain that turned day into night: the bee. The bee was also lovely to behold, and it provided of pleasure, because flowers come from bees just as honey does.

The bee made that endless journey shorter, straighter. The white darkness of those spores was no longer necessary, it was superfluous. Flowers blossomed in abundance and fruit trees sprang up.

Mushrooms despised the bee from the beginning.

Humans could once again see light without that cloudy, white curtain, and breathe deeply. The horizon reappeared, as if Earth had suddenly returned to a manageable size.

After trying and succeeding with a variety of different creatures, Eve thought of creating us, and that's how you were born, Cain, the first human, my brother and my husband, my protector and the one I protect, my companion and joy, and my misfortune.

ANOTHER DAUGHTER OF EVE:
This is what Eve told me. It's her truth:

One day she found an oyster that was much larger than the others at the bottom of the riverbank; it was rounder, more opulent, the grooves on its shell much deeper and darker. The other oysters looked so small and pale that Eve didn't hesitate to pick it up.

Eve told me, "It must have been the first of its species, like I was." In her eyes this was the Eve-oyster.

Her comment annoyed me. I was better than her previous creations, conceived by her—by Eve, without any help—and I didn't want to hear it anymore. As if she was reading my mind, she added, "There was something surprising about that oyster; it was heavy like it held a large pearl, a pearl of solid metal. But the oyster itself looked light as gold, though it was thicker than the others."

Eve put the oyster in a bowl. She poured the juice of three lemons over it. And doused it with salt and water, along with some fragrant herbs, the kind that are so tough they're impossible to chew. She put it on the fire.

The oyster opened a little, surrounded and protected by the herbs, but looking as if it would devour them in the blink of an eye.

Eve took the two halves of this vulva between her thumbs and revealed all its secrets. Inside there was no mollusk, but a strange animal with a long body. It had not shrunk from simmering in the lemon-herb broth and its colors had brightened. It appeared to be able to speak.

87

"I want to make something clear: back then no one had spoken yet. We said words, but it wasn't really speaking . . ."

She described to me what came out of that oyster. The creature looked a bit like an octopus. When she took it out of the shell, fully cooked but very much alive, she saw it had tentacles with suction cups. She touched it. The creature reacted; one of its arms wrapped around her finger. And she understood what the creature was saying to her:

"Let's make monsters."

That was the beginning of the era of monsters, Eve said. Giant creatures that devoured anything that moved.

They even ate the wind. Fog sprang up in its place. The monsters began to devour each other, eating each other in the darkness. Next, they ate light. They ate so much that when one of them passed gas, or something similar, it became light again.

Eve fled from the sight of what those monsters had done. She was unable to describe the wasteland she saw before her escape.

ANOTHER:
Eve fled toward the sea. She was afraid of the water, expecting it to harbor countless oysters that were home to creatures who would birth more monsters with her blessing. She was keenly aware that she had been an accomplice to the birth of those voracious monsters.

Then, Eve told me, for the first time in her life, she cried. Those were the first tears on Earth, though she tells a different story today.

ANOTHER:
(And Eve said: "Let's make monsters!" And she who shapes all things brought to life snakes and monsters with pitiless jaws.)

BOOK THREE

BOOK THREE

24

Descent

We descended the high, steep peaks (from the first and most inaccessible one to other rugged, steep summits), moving through a forest of jagged slopes.

Looking back, I recall walking along calmly; it would have been impossible to proceed with confidence if we had known the extreme dangers we faced, we would have been blinded by fear. On the contrary, our lack of awareness lighted our way, giving Adam and me a kind of sustenance, enabling us to carry on.

I focused on the magnificent spread of Earth below us, and not on what stood between us and it: though it appeared insignificant from the summit, the labyrinth of peaks that surrounded the Divine Mount was vast: an incredibly high, extensive rampart with exceptionally tall, crude towers. Apart from the ridges and hidden resting places I have described, there were also plateaus between the slopes where we enjoyed Earth's gifts during our descent.

It was clear that jumping from peak to peak to descend the jagged mountain range was no small feat, and we had undertaken it blindly, underestimating its difficulty.

As previously mentioned, some of those hunks of rock and stone held water, and it was in those places that we found great solace. We carried the embers in the angel-stone like a treasure, and our thirst like a curse.

Formidable birds appeared to swing back and forth in the air, and their chicks cheeped in nooks and crannies of the cliffs. Large goats scattered when they saw us approach. A tribe of violent, hostile apes stalked us, cutting off our passage again and again. Copying the Angel, we scared them away by throwing stones at them, then we had to run to make it past them. For long stretches we carried torches to keep them at bay, and as we descended the torches shielded us from other wild animals, too.

25

The Rivulet of Water

It must have been two full days since we had left the sanctuary when we came across a lively rivulet of water that burst forth from a rocky slope. First, we quenched our thirst; the stream of water slithered down the slope, becoming a frothy brook, so we decided to follow its course.

As we progressed the white brook swelled, becoming wider, its volume seeming to flow with greater urgency; it shed the white crests it had donned earlier and became clear, accompanied by little fish, tadpoles, and other creatures, some close to its banks, others leaping against the current or seeming to rest in it.

The river paid us no attention, but not so its inhabitants; all we had to do was put our hands in the water or cast our shadows on its surface for them to withdraw in disgust. More birds (long legged ones) and sly animals (those goats with large horns, the cats that stalked them) approached the river to drink as we descended the slope alongside it; the animals also fled from us, and if they didn't at first, they did when we shook our torches at them.

Suddenly, the river disappeared from view. Underground. We continued our descent following the swath of green that marked its underground passage, as it moistened the earth covering it, germinating seeds. Here and there small springs of water bubbled up, but not like the original one—these had no strength and were tinged the color of the dark earth; we drank from them since we had no alternative, and on the days it rained we drank raindrops from leaves like little green pots.

26

The Cave-House; Making Fire; The Song;
The First Cave Painting; The End of Our Hooves

It rained nonstop. When the rain was accompanied by freezing wind we sheltered in the nooks and crannies of that mountain range surrounding the Divine Mount, to save the embers we were carrying inside the angel-stone and because since we were naked when the temperature dropped the cold was more bearable if we sheltered.

On one of these occasions, we found ourselves in a cavern. Our discovery coincided with a long period of rain; although it was hardly Paradise, we settled down there. It was our first home.

In the cave we were safe from bears, apes, leopards, and other beasts, even without torches. No longer hounded, we tried to find a way to relieve the chafing on our worn hooves.

They had provided good traction and made us sure-footed, but we had walked so far that parts of our feet had become exposed. The worn edges of our hooves were hurting us. We filed them down using rough, flat stones. After that all that was left of them were rings around our ankles.

It was our need to smooth the sharp edges of what was left of our hooves that made Adam build our first fire in that cave, because he wanted to sharpen the edge of one of the slates we used to carry the fire (a rough stone, it was ideal for filing), so he rubbed it against the white wall of the cave. The black slate resisted, but its friction with the white stone produced a spark.

Adam scraped it along the stone wall and sparks flew. He did it again and again, delighted. I moved close to the sparks that were falling: they burned. I took a handful of dried grass we had saved and, extending my arms, put them near the sparks: they caught the burning spark. I put them on the ground, breathing on them gently, and Adam fed them with more dried grass and twigs: we built a fire.

We rejoiced. We continued to blow on the flames to encourage them. Our breath, accompanied by the repetition of long vowels exhaled softly by our mouths and noses—monotone *las*—rang musically in the cave, a song.

My face trembled, and the air that made it tremble was also refreshing, in contrast to the heat of the burning grass. Adam joined my song—with a *do*—holding his breath in his palate before exhaling slowly.

The effect of our voices on our fire made sparks jump in our faces. The fire grew and our shadows grew along with it, as did our astonishment at this new phenomenon. We continued making sounds—*la, do,* nose, palate, throat—without allowing the pitches we had each chosen to falter or break, as if it was the only dependable thing in this rather magical place that did not seem to be on Earth, but instead at its very core.

We sat and crossed our legs in front of this fire that did not come from what we had taken from the Angel—a fire made with our own sparks (from the stone, the cave, and our hands)—in a state of joyful peace. We clapped our hands.

Adam left the fire and began to climb the wall of the cave, placing his feet in the crevices. He held the stone the Angel had thrown at me in one hand. He knew we no longer needed it to have fire. Imitating a vulture, he threw it to the floor of the cave to break it. He only succeeded in splitting one of the edges, breaking off two pieces of crystal from the inside, which I saved.

At first, we were frightened by the shapes our shadows made on the walls of the house-cave, but they soon made us laugh, entertaining us. We fed the fire with new branches, learning how to make our shadows larger or smaller. The fire from these new branches ended up completely covering the wall of the cave closest to the fire in soot.

One night I scraped the soot with one of the crystals Adam broke off the angel-stone; I drew a line and above it I traced a simple figure: the outline of a woman's torso. I drew a perpendicular line across it, representing her arms, and I sketched two more vertical lines downward, her legs.

The contrast of the white rock beneath the velvety black soot was so stark, it looked like the figure had been traced in white on black. Beside it I scraped another vertical line and traced two wings like the ones I thought I saw on the Angel of light, and when I filled them in to make them white sparks began to fly: the Angel was made of light.

Then I returned to the first figure and added two hooves at the bottom of its legs, enormous compared to the rest of the body, hooves that would endure the longest of journeys. I filled them in, too, and they also produced sparks.

I produced light just like the Angel's with those sparks, but I did it my own way, creating light by touching and rubbing. In my drawing I showed how we scratched at our hooves after so much walking the Earth, and I traced our fire with the tip of the crystal.

As soon as the storm cleared up, we continued on our way, freed from the burden of carrying the fire, since we knew how to make it—but I didn't leave a single piece of the angel-stone behind.

What little remained of our hooves wore away.

27

Curiosity, Fear, Cooking

We wanted to see, come to know, and live on the immense Earth, which we had first glimpsed from the highest peak of the range of the Divine Mount. Adam was gradually losing his fearfulness and his worries; he had joined me in curiosity, which was our oar and our sail.

We were wrought of resilient stuff, like the fig leaves that protected the embers for many months. As we were losing our hooves our muscles grew stronger. Our tendons, tauter. Light and wiry, we moved ever more swiftly, following the sinuous gully downward until it became a river.

Now that I think of it, at that time my Adam was like my little one, my puppy dog; not like a boy, more like a little kid who clung to me for protection, retaining some of his old fearfulness. He laughed less than I did, but he did laugh. He would take risks if he was following me, and he was the one who created the spark once he gained some confidence, as I said. I'm explaining his behavior because I depicted our origins on the wall of that cave and though he thought of me as the fire-keeper, in truth we both were.

And there was something else: he was terrified of getting in the water. At first, I had waded in up to my waist, then my breasts, my shoulders, my head. I learned to swim in the spots where the river became still and later, I ventured out into the current. I saw the world beneath its surface. I learned about fish and other aquatic life. Adam, on the other hand, avoided water unless it was to drink; he didn't dare get in.

I often slept on the riverbank, where the water would cover me when it rose; on those occasions he preferred to sleep alone—which he hated—to avoid the risk.

I wasn't a passive swimmer; I swam with and against the current, floating and diving under. I found all kinds of oysters for us to eat, some large, some small. On the fire I roasted plants that grew on shells and swayed like animals (though it was obvious they weren't), sea urchins (which I learned to open), and other water creatures that did not have eyes like we did; I also toasted fruits, herbs, leaves, stalks, and roots. Just like in my first dream, the fire extracted new smells and scents from them, transforming their flavor, delighting us, making our meals delicious. It wasn't even close to the apple I had tasted in Eden, but fragrant and tasty, nonetheless.

After many days of rain and cold, the sky cleared up and we continued our descent.

28

Fingernails, Hair. One Anus, the Other, Defecation and Hunger

My hair grew capriciously. My fingernails grew long. The ones on my toes began to stick out and became sharp, instead of growing over my feet like our hooves had (though they were a similar material).

One night when Adam and I were sleeping soundly together, I poked a hole at the base of his spine with my thumbnail. The pain of the tear woke him up; a kind of pulp came out of the crack, what his body didn't need, and immediately Adam felt relieved.

This involuntary act marked the beginning of a new era. The tear had an effect on his appetite; he no longer felt only thirst, but also hunger.

The accident showed me that he had a certain wisdom, that for all his wildness he was not an idiot, he was gifted with knowledge that extended beyond himself. It also showed me to be more attentive to what was happening.

My fingernails helped me do everything. They were, I can now say, my most useful tools. I used my thumbnail to make a tear at the base of my own spine, releasing everything my body didn't want, and I felt the same relief Adam had experienced. And hunger.

Inspired by my fingernails, I carved the two slates into our first tools. I carved them, put them away, and looked after them, and I even filed my fingernails and combed my hair, decorating it with feathers.

29

To the Plains, the Beasts, the Clay

We continued the journey downward. It was less arduous, the plant life more abundant, the cold seemed to have stayed behind, and we arrived upon a golden plateau that looked like it extended to the ends of the universe. It was joined by the river, which flowed freely and suddenly branched into three wide, uncrossable branches.

Along the sides of this wide river animals abounded. The apes we had seen up above, or ones like them, existed here in great numbers. We kept our distance, which wasn't difficult because they were so noisy, we could easily hear them coming.

Animals of considerable size appeared in the river, too, like the hippopotami, which were always in groups. Gazelles, elephants, giraffes, and a multitude of birds. Most shied away from us, while some of the larger ones ignored us; the rest considered us prey, like the leopards in the treetops, lying in wait.

One of the branches of the river was full of little, gnarled islands that looked like birds' nests made of sticks, branches, husks, feathers, rings of sand, and whatever else was to be found, surrounded by rushing waters, and some were ornamented by living plants that had plenty of water to blossom.

I recall that there was a hungry gazelle on one of these swiftly floating islands; traveling thus, it was free from attack by larger beasts, but it could hardly take a single step, sailing along in that wide river, looking like a tempting feast. It would likely die of hunger if it wasn't eaten by a crocodile first.

30

Molding Clay, the Conversation

The river: water and food, guide and protector and threat. Without warning it overflowed, bursting its banks, expanding impetuously, flooding the plateau, and turning it into a swamp. It might drag us away or devour us on a whim, cut us off, or deliver us to the jaws of a ravenous beast.

We decided to follow its course from a distance. In the earth that was left behind after it swelled and receded, I noticed that the mud became dry and hardened like stone, mapping its previous course. This river-earth was malleable when wet and hard when it dried.

I took a few fistfuls of it and tried to shape it with my hands while it was sticky. It was impossible. I added some shells that I ground up using nearby stones, some coarse sand from the high part of the plain, and some lime which I had found along the way, to create a kind of dough I formed into shapes, without any purpose at first.

I tried to copy the appearance and shape of the things that mattered most to me, from the angel-stone to the apple (which looked more like a fig) to my body and parts of Adam's. Then I molded a vessel for holding water.

In this state the clay was still wet and porous and did not hold water. I molded the clay in different shapes to see if it would hold water for longer. I let them dry in the sun. No matter how often I tried, varying the proportion of shells and lime and different kinds of sand, they remained fragile and porous.

I wet fistfuls of clay repeatedly, continuing to shape it into cups, wrapping it in straw and immersing it in the flames of that sheltering sun, the fire which I fed constantly.

Then I let the cup dry. It had become hard. It held water for longer. I made two more cups, one for Adam, one for me. They were for drinking. I made a fourth shape, a pot, and I fired them all. The cups performed their duty. I put the tough, multicolored branches of a sweet-smelling bush into the pot, which I placed on the coals. They attained a different, pleasant flavor.

I continued to work with the clay. I mixed it with bits of straw. I dug a pit to contain the fire. I cooked these vessels beneath the coals (burying them to sustain the heat). After letting them cool, first on the dying coals, then in the open air, the cups held water even better, if not completely.

By this time Adam and I were able to have a conversation, using words derived from others; we had verbs, and our speech had become more complex. That was when we began to notice the passage of time; we measured it by the movement of the Sun and the stars; we gave names and numbers to the days.

END OF BOOK THREE

Loose papers from the pages of Book Three

ON THE RUN:
Many times, we escaped being eaten or enslaved by the wild beasts. We struggled to figure out what we could put in our mouths without vomiting, becoming dizzy, or feeling ill. I didn't do this intentionally; I lack the necessary instincts. We had brought the goal of protecting ourselves and surviving with us from mute Eden, because we yearned to be outside of Time.

Although I lived all this it's not my thing. Mine is roasting apples, cooking vegetables, browning and toasting seeds, finding the flavor in the food we had to eat. But eating or being eaten is a basic question that exceeds the limits of our grammar: it's part of nature. But I'm not really part of nature, no one is. There's something in us that doesn't come from Earth, that makes us yearn for it and desire it, knowing we have different roots. Which is why we invent things to belong to—countries, creeds, and more. We'll never fully belong to this paradise or hell we inhabit.

ANOTHER PAPER:
We hurled the geode that the Angel had thrown at me, breaking it into tiny pieces of quartz, which we tossed into the sky to return fate's gift to us, so that it would pay us back with other gifts.

BOOK FOUR

31

The Wellspring with Light: Our Refuge

Recounting all the threats we faced and our subsequent escapes would be tedious, like listing the things we ate before we discovered the plateau, and it would also be absurd, relative to the multitude of gifts Earth presents. I'll describe just one, the wellspring with light.

We found a place that gave us full protection from the wild animals. It was a rocky ravine that shone like an arid, hostile hill from afar. Even the birds didn't dare nest in its high, nearly vertical walls. It looked impenetrable, as if it were made of solid stone. But at its center, which could be reached only by a single, narrow, labyrinthine path, was a lush wellspring. We settled there. We closed the narrow entrance with a huge boulder that we patiently hauled into place to shelter from the beasts.

That place was lit even at night; the light that shone from the wellspring refracted in the shadows. Splashing or stirring the water filled the place with luminous blue-green light with metallic glints.

No longer did we have to run, nor did we want to. There was nothing to flee. The river couldn't reach us. And our refuge had its own climate, neither hot nor cold.

Two small bushes blossomed, and their flowers became fruits similar to pomegranates, deep red and delicious. Delicate greenery surrounded the pond. Honeybees buzzed. We watched them tirelessly building the honeycomb, their home.

Our refuge was our own private paradise.

32

The Smoke and the Bees, the Honey. Another Dream of Eve's

Out of curiosity I put a burning pile of fresh branches next to the bees' home. The smoke startles them. Suddenly they all fly away. I look at the honeycomb. I leave, and when the smoke dissipates the bees return to work.

The next day I approach the honeycomb again with my smoking, fresh branches and when the bees leave, I steal a piece of their home. I taste their delicious honey and invite Adam to as well; I chew the sticky wax of the comb, so different from the apple. When all its flavor is gone, I keep the wax, molding it and bringing it with me.

The same day that I steal the honey, I dream that Adam and I make love in a way: he is a hyena, I'm a cadaver.

33

The Seed of Paradise

When I awaken, troubled by my dream, I need to take a walk. Adam sleeps, muttering something or other. I stir the waters of the pond to illuminate the night. I don't go near the beehive, I move as far away from it as I do from Adam, keeping them both in my sight.

I'm standing. Contemplating the sky. I see the high walls of stone surrounding me, protecting us. I pick a small stone off the ground and throw it into the pond, the water is sprinkled with stars, so different from and so similar to the brightness in the heavens.

I'm still standing. As I often do, I remove the apple seed—the one I took from the tree with the delicious fruit in Eden—which I keep in the thick hair that grows under my arm. I look at the sky once more. I brush the smooth seed against my lips. And do it again.

I'm still standing. Looking at the sky. I don't know why I put the seed in my mouth and swallow it with my saliva.

I close my eyes. I feel the seed move silently through me, timidly at first, cautious, until the nearby sound of my heart enlivens it. Then, due to inertia more than gravity, it becomes astral, faster than anything inside a body, animated by my internal beat, spurred on by the movement of my blood and the humors of my liver. I notice the vertigo with which it moves through me; it avoids the waste excreted through my rear. The tiny thing travels all the way to the lowest part of my thorax, the place between my legs, which is like an endless passage that has only one exit, for urine. But the seed doesn't take the exit. It's moving freely inside my body. And what is mine belongs to it, too.

I feel its impact inside me, it's moving outward. I feel it split me in two. It's almost out of my body. But then it's not, stopped by the arch at the base of my trunk. And then it starts rising again, back the way it came, all the way to the center of my chest. I breathe deeply. The air I inhale is breathed by the seed, too, and it takes flight. Next it dives precipitously to the arch between my legs.

This time its impact is so great that its sweet point opens a new passage between my legs.

"Legs that stand upon earth," it seems the seed is saying, speaking to them through the passage that has just opened, "be alert." My legs buckle. I squat. And at the center of that new passageway, the clitoris blossoms: the vivid pleasure of the apple breaking and opening my skin. Raw flesh, sensitive, wise to the heart, intimate of blood, aware of earthly gravity, both rigid and soft, it contained both the word and the memory of the intense pleasure I felt when I bit into the fruit, as well as an awareness of myself, and more, much more.

I moved my hand to my clitoris.

That first bite that crunched between my teeth and changed our lives had reserved for me, in that little black seed, the ultimate pleasure.

34

The Clitoris

Clitoris, apple, fire, seed: the comparisons are limited, but here are three.

One involves the apple. They say I gave the apple to Adam to taste it. If we take that as a given (as I'm doing), we'd know without a doubt that Adam felt something like what I did, although less intensely—his wasn't a lesser experience, but it was attenuated, reduced, his pleasure wasn't comparable to mine.

The second involves fire, which the handsome Angel held, making me long for it, and which I obtained, giving us day in the night, our anchor against the storms of nightly fear, our protection from the wild beasts. It would never have occurred to Adam to flirt with the Angel or steal it.

The third involves the seed. Aware of what the apple seed had given me—opening me up to the clitoris—I enjoyed touching myself.

Adam awoke and realized there was something different about me. I was still touching my clitoris, in ecstasy. Adam stirred the water in the luminous pond to get a better look at me. He regarded me coldly, scrutinizing me. Perhaps he was remembering the apple, but I'm certain that he wanted what I had. He didn't know how I had gotten it, so he made a simple attempt: he took my hand off my clitoris and put it between his legs. But there was nothing there. He didn't feel a thing. I took my hand back.

And it wasn't just that night. I touched my clitoris constantly; the pleasure was always there, waiting for me. Adam wanted to imitate me, to have what I had. He had noticed that my hand wasn't the source of the sensation, so he tried with his own. And he kept on trying.

Determined, he rubbed and rubbed and kept on rubbing the space between his legs, even trying with other objects, but he couldn't obtain the delightful feeling I had been gifted by the seed of that delicious fruit, made incarnate inside my body, manifesting outside it.

Adam rubbed so much that he created a fold in the skin between his legs.

35

The Seeds, the Flower, an Angel, and Another

Among other things, I understood the importance of seeds because my clitoris was born from the apple seed. And I had no doubt that my clitoris would not have blossomed if I had not been on Earth.

So, I learned to revere seeds, associating them with Earth. I learned to see them, touch them, tell them apart, collect them, sow them and look after them. I understood that I needed to use my hands with the Earth to bend them to my will.

I chose a seed that had an orange tip and whose surface was relatively smooth. I made it a bed: scraping together some earth, watering it, and placing the seed there, covering it with a little more earth. I marked the place with some small stones and sand. I made sure it didn't lack water. I watched it and cared for it.

Adam watched me doing this, but he didn't copy me, he just kept on pulling the flap of skin that had appeared between his legs without achieving anything other than making that flap of skin a little longer.

When my seed sprouted its first green bud an angel appeared, not a fiery one, but one made of light. A gorgeous angel, unbearably gorgeous, like that first Angel of fire, the guardian of Eden. It was a witness angel. The stalk grew and produced a bud, and the bud opened and flowered, an intense red color with little orange spots in its center. The Angel observed and left. It had come just to witness its birth.

A bee visited my flower. It drank and buzzed away.

The flower didn't last long. It made me sad to see its petals lose their color and shrivel. It pained me to see each petal fall.

I searched for a similar seed.

I won't go into detail: a series of brightly colored flowers blossomed, with visitations from the Angel of light and then other angels—as if each flower had a partner-angel.

The bees arrived in number, going from flower to flower.

One of these flowers produced a fruit for me, a kind of squash that crunched between my teeth, almost like that apple in Eden. Adam was nowhere to be seen, and I couldn't share the fruit with him.

The white darkness of the spores that had fallen annually and had been washed away by the rain, ceased. The bees supplanted it when they pollinated the flowers.

36

Clitoris Envy. The Penis

I didn't forget about my clitoris for a single moment, how could I have?

With regard to Adam, as I already explained, when my clitoris first appeared, and I experienced its pleasure, he had created a fold in the skin between his legs. It hung there, inert. Completely useless.

Adam observed my pleasure the same way he observed me making the cups—without joining the party. He watched me and watched some more. Watching stirred something in him, perhaps it was a corollary to what I felt when I was using clay to make things that we used day to day . . . When he watched me touch my clitoris, something stirred in him in the same way. Watching was becoming part of who he was—he was turning into a pair of eyes, increasingly passive.

His presence began to annoy me, but I couldn't just leave him. Aware of my annoyance, and unsatisfied, his gaze became dull.

Intuition saved us.

One afternoon, after a long laugh about something that's not important, when I put my hand on my clitoris and I saw Adam's expression change, I moved my hand to his flap of skin, the one he had made by constantly rubbing between his legs. I rubbed and rubbed and rubbed and rubbed. I rubbed and kept on rubbing.

The front tail that had been hanging sleepily between his legs awoke. The dullness of his gaze cleared. He moved my hand aside. He started rubbing and rubbing himself, urging that little tail to grow. It grew and grew. That little tail became a bigger tail and then a long hanging thing.

As the days passed, with all that constant rubbing, the thing took on a life of its own, it appeared to stop jiggling and swell a bit, and then more, until it was nearly the size of Adam's hand. The swelling didn't last.

The thing hanging between his legs, a mere parody of what we'd later refer to as his sword, stood up. But how? Was that also caused by Adam's envy of my own pleasure?

Because I had everything I needed for pleasure: I had a clitoris.

But whenever he stopped rubbing his thing it became a limp tail again, dangling. Adam kept on rubbing until his tail pointed up toward the sky. He was determined to continue rubbing to keep it upright, employing various tools to help rub or sheathe his erect dangler. He wanted to keep it erect no matter what else he needed to do with his hands, in ferocious pursuit of the pleasure that came so effortlessly and simply to me, all mine.

Adam was feeling clitoris envy. Males will always have it, that unspoken, unexpressed envy of the clitoris. The silence that accompanies this envy makes it all the more apparent.

Our relationship changed because of this resentment. It had some positive effects: Adam got his hands dirty with clay, making his first cup. When he finished it, Adam's gaze was clear once more, pure.

37

We Poison Our Refuge

We poisoned our refuge. The wellspring with light originated as droplets (not as a constant stream) in the bowels of the Earth; most of its volume came from those accumulated droplets and from rainwater. It naturally gave off light. We stirred its waters for a long while when the Sun set, to refract its brightness in the darkness of night. We kept its waters moving to awaken the light, disturb its peace, prevent the underwater source of light from stilling.

Whatever was creating the light (bacteria, fungi, some other organism), we disrupted its happy isolation, spreading disturbance throughout the water, making the water undrinkable. Whatever had made it emit light was ruined when we began stirring the waters nightly, causing it to proliferate throughout the wellspring.

We removed the giant stone we had used to block the entrance to the rocky ravine, preparing to leave our refuge and go in search of water we could drink (I gathered germinated seeds, adding them to our bundle of tools, of which my favorite was my first comb, carved from a piece of dry tree trunk) when a huge lion[4] appeared, voracious and immense. It was preceded by a gigantic flying creature.

---

4. An enormous, extinct animal with a mane, yet not so similar to a modern lion.

Facing these two beasts, we thought our lives were over. We ran to the fire where we were in the process of preparing our torches and set them ablaze, brandishing them: the flying creature disappeared from sight and the giant lion retreated; we cornered it in a hole in the rocks at the bottom of the ravine, planting three torches there to keep it at bay, roaring but paralyzed.

We cautiously rushed away, leaving behind some of the most beautiful seeds I had planted. I had that mouthful of wax from the honeycomb I stole from the bees stuck in my navel. We both carried a torch in one hand, like our own guardian angels.

Soon enough our thirst compelled us to approach the riverbank, where the wild animals lay in wait, eyeing the meat on our bones. We didn't put our torches down for a second, we held our blazing shields tight, and especially when we stopped to rest along our way.

END OF BOOK FOUR

Loose pages

ONE:
"And Adam, Eve? What about Adam?"

"A little, Adam."

"Eve! Why just a little?"

"Listen: my soul had only just come into existence. I couldn't tell things apart very well, Adam included, what was more this than that, more inanimate than Adam, and since I couldn't tell . . ."

ANOTHER:
That's not how the clitoris came to be part of the female body. When they came to the plateau where the equatorial sun unleashes its full power, Eve thought she would suffocate. She swallowed the seed—magical thinking: just like the apple, it would give her new life. The seed, which was also overheated and agitated, went down her throat, though rather against its will because in Eve's mouth it sensed that in the dark, crimson interior of her body it was even more stifling. Even more than under her arm, and inside there was no nest where it could rest comfortably, like the one made by her underarm hair.

It fought through intestine, muscle, and bone to find a way out. The seed took charge. But it couldn't figure out how to escape from the Eve-oven. It moved around, ever more frenetically, until it bumped into Eve's heart and broke it. The seed was lost, and Eve was crestfallen, but the former gathered its strength and, taking advantage of gravity, hurtled rapidly toward the base of her abdomen. The rest (how the clitoris blossomed, etcetera) is common knowledge, and Eve was happy, complete.

Though there are those who say that things were the other way around—from outside in, like Adam's penis—that since the heat made the seed's hideaway in Eve's underarm hair unbearable, it slid down her side and turned around at the base of her abdomen, brushing the area between her legs and there, between her legs, it pushed into her body *against* the force of gravity, managing to travel from her lower abdomen to her heart, lungs, and brain, linking them all to the clitoris.

ANOTHER:

I continued gathering seeds and leaves (from the delicious fruit and from the fig tree, to cover ourselves and to tend the fire, burning them), just as I had done with words. I soon had a collection of dried branches, stalks, grasses, leaves, flowers, roots, fungi; their scent intrigued me, or I was curious about them, or I used them to feed the fire I continued to carry, or we ate them because, though I think it's unnecessary to specify, I was eager to taste different flavors—the delicious fruit from Eden had awakened me, opened me to tasting things. My palate wanted to know, to try, and to enjoy.

The palate. What a word. Mine in a way the word death will never be, or even that gruff word: mine. Mine: you, "my" word, are not mine.

I harbored no illusion that a different seed would open a different mouth in my body. It was unnecessary: I knew that the clitoris, which the black, shiny seed I took from the tree of the forbidden fruit had gifted me, was unique. Though that's not the right word: each one of the many different sensations that great source of pleasure gave me was forever unique—that word was and always will be mine, as much mine as my clitoris is, was, and will be, till death do us part. Although in my case death is but a word . . .

ANOTHER:

I dreamed, night after night I dreamed. My dreams, grown and prepared by me (like the food we ate), intertwined, gathering meaning, narrating, and weaving together: through them I learned that my life was a story, or better said, a series of stories that, when put together, became endowed with meaning. Like the life of a plant has a sensible order: seed, root, stalk, bud, leaf, flower, fruit.

And what about the apple?

BOOK FIVE

38

The River's Mud and Its Beasts

The river gifted us its mud and the fertility of the soil it had previously watered, but it also attracted the wild animals. Of course, if we carried fire or set it down near us, we were able to keep them at bay, but surges in the river's flow made it impossible to always keep it burning.

And then there was the fact that the swampy land alongside it was uninhabitable, largely due to the elusive and treacherous creatures that lived there, many of which were poisonous.

When the river rose it was dangerous, it swelled unpredictably and rapidly, flooding everything in its path—sometimes as far as the eye could see—attempting to devour us along with the trunks and dead beasts it had swallowed as it broke its banks. Once, we were saved only by a tree with a huge ball of roots whose branches kept us from being swept away. Adam and I held fast to its gnarled branches until the river receded within its banks.

We moved away from the river, putting distance between it and us. Once again, we experienced thirst. We made use of dried fruits (gourds) to gather water as we proceeded, tying them together with plant fibers we wove each night by the heat of the fire. We also made use of the remains of animals we encountered along the way. Bladders for holding liquid; bones, especially jawbones, as useful tools; teeth to protect us from the spirits of the night.

We also gathered animals' hooves, along with their tendons

and strips of their hide, to tie our receptacles together, among other things.

And all this was good: generous Earth provided for us in so many ways.

39

The Stink of Sulfur, the Rescue, Our Fence, the House-Tent

Perhaps we would have ended up being eaten by the beasts or died of hunger and thirst if we had not discovered a hideaway in the savanna which was ideal for settling down. There was a stench about it that other creatures found repugnant; it was a long, narrow ravine shaped like a V, its sharp angles appearing to rise out of the bowels of the Earth, a deep gully at the bottom.

The air around the ravine was unbreathable. It stank like a mound of burnt hair and irritated the lungs, causing nausea. Its foul-smelling gases were asphyxiating. Out of its depths on the far side of the gully a strong, steady wind blew, carrying the foul smells the ravine exuded toward the savanna.

In its cloudy, ill-smelling waters a few fish surfaced, their mouths gaping in desperation, as if they were trying to find air to breathe, sticking their huge heads out of the water constantly, determined to survive. Their bodies were slim and feeble, insignificant compared to their heads, and they were transparent, revealing their innards. They were as revolting as the hair-raising waters of the ravine, an awful home.

Lines formed along the black sand banks of the gully, alternating off-white and dark green, and in places closer to the waterline piles of slimy, slippery stones accumulated.

Not a single wild animal could bear to approach the foul ravine.

The fish that lived there must have been souls that received Beelzebub's harshest punishment.

We plugged our nostrils with beeswax. We picked a spot that didn't have stones along the bank and jumped across the stinking stream. The vegetation grew thick on that side. We entered the thicket. Twenty steps away, a natural spring bubbled into view, its fresh waters sparkling and perfectly clear, feeding a pond filled with a multitude of brightly colored fish larger than our arms, fat fish with strong bodies and small, discreet mouths—uninterested in approaching the surface of the pond.

At the bottom of this pond lay perfectly round stones, even more brightly colored than the fish. They would soon prove especially useful for starting fires when struck against the fragments of the pieces of the stone I had carried all the way from the slopes of the Divine Mount.

Past the pond, on the edge of the cliff where this stretch of land ended, a row of thick trees grew close together, their sparse, dark leaves sprouting from stunted branches that had grown together to create a fluttering curtain that couldn't stop the wind, allowing the protective stench of our ravine, which lay just beyond, to blow away, creating a warm, stable climate. The wind blew steadily from the depths, as if the throat of the Earth were trying to speak to us.

Between these trees and the long, fetid, V-shaped gully, there was a triangular area covered in vibrant light green vegetation—huge leaves, some of which were long and thin while others were so broad that three of them side by side could cover the whole area. Along the edges of this triangle flanked by the stinking ravine we dug two trenches, which we covered with grass: traps for the beasts, the work of our own hands, using bone shovels and sticks. They would stop the vermin but not the larger animals; for that we relied on the strength of the stench and the protection of the

128

ravine. Leopards, our greatest threat, would be unable to scale the rickety branches that grew straight up from the tree-fence, parallel to their trunks—they were too thin and would crumble under any weight.

As far as insects were concerned, there was nothing to worry about, whether they had wings or not. Not many would figure out how to avoid the stench and navigate the winds from the ravine.

Weaving fibers from the plants that grew along the path from the spring to the pond, we made fabric for a tent to shelter us. We used sturdy, pliable sticks from the bald trees that screened the ravine to hold it up. It proved to be a reliable, protective roof. In time we learned to weave the fibers more closely together and our tent completely shielded us from the rain.

The large trees were a species of sterile fruit tree that never bore the fruit they were meant to grow. Barren as they were, they proved of great use to us, because they gave us poles for chairs and a table.

When we succeeded in weaving more durable fabric, we remade our tent and were fully protected from the rain.

The stinking, protective ravine had other virtues. When exposed to heat, the sticky, slimy, slippery green stones turned red, as if they were on fire, and became malleable, like clay. It was impossible to touch them when they were so hot, so I tried to put them in one of my bigger cups to cool.

40

The Kitchen: Keeping Track of Time, the Pursuit of Pleasure, Decoration

Fire evolved from protection against the darkness into the focal point of our gatherings together and our meals. At the same time, we began to make clothes from leaves I dried with the flames.

Settled at last, we began to keep track of the days. We drew lines on the huge, ancient trunk of one of the trees, marking the passage of time with stones.

But the most reliable and unforgiving measure was the fireplace where food was cooked and seasoned—I began to play around with our food. Mere seconds determined whether the flavor and texture of our food was disgusting, palatable, or delicious. Fire had different effects on food. Nothing could be recreated or prepared the same way twice, depending on whether the fruits, flowers, grasses, or roots were out of season or fresh. Which is how I learned that time cannot be measured in lines or marks; it's an unstable thing, like light.

We ate from wooden bowls we hollowed out with tools carved from stone. We built two seats with legs that matched the size of our own from our knees to the ground; they were chairs, really.

Using colors we extracted from fruits and seeds before and after heating them up, we painted our skin. Covered in a variety of shapes and marks, there was no part of my body that was not embellished with color, and most of Adam's was, too.

To arrange my long hair, I carved a comb (as I have already mentioned) and then I carved more, including smaller ones to hold my hair up. When it was combed smooth, my hair was silken, like something from another world. Nothing is more unlike the virgin Earth than silky hair.

I cleaned my teeth with sand. If my nails grew uncomfortably long, I filed them down with a rough stone. I made necklaces out of flowers, and short skirts out of dried leaves. Adam preferred to be completely naked, whereas I enjoyed adorning myself.

I also painted our cups and cooking pots.

I think now that I learned to want to adorn my body from the trees, which do so each passing day, changing their leaves, shedding blossom, releasing spores that adorn the sky.

41

Wanting Children. First Attempts

Of course, I had seen wild animals laying eggs or giving birth to their young. But Adam and I were certain that we were a different species, our origins were different, which is why our teeth and our bones were so similar. We didn't know where the wild animals came from, but we knew we came from the bite of the apple.

The animals? They weren't like the creatures that Thunder had forced to be silent. Back in Eden, there had been no creepy-crawlies, no vermin, no beasts like the enormous beings we kept running into ever since the river had become a force to reckon with.

But the size of the beasts wasn't as important as the way the insects (and vermin) provided food for all the other creatures. The birds ate them. The fish ate the small aquatic ones. The small animals ate them, too. And the large animals ate the small ones, and the fish and the birds.

The aquatic life, the airborne, the earthbound, the creatures that slithered along and the ones that lived underground all produced their young with their own bodies, and if that weren't revolting enough—to the clear-eyed procreation is like self-cannibalization, it's repulsive, the inverse of cannibalism—they ate vermin, too. Without a doubt, we wouldn't follow the same method as them, that much was obvious: one cannot produce a child alone, much less "bleed" or "excrete" or "urinate" it out, or, as they say, "give birth."

The arrival of a person on Earth cannot culminate in defecation or expulsion through some other orifice, like the elimination of uncomfortable, built-up gas. That is not what we are and we put this into words since we're no longer condemned to lack language for eternity.

I mention this here because of what follows.

42

I Tell Our History on Stone, Adam Tells His Lie

As a gesture of trust, friendship, understanding, and brotherhood, Adam gave me his half of the seed. I put it in my mouth and united it with my half, making it one, like pre-chewed food for a young child.

Of course: the mouth. The apple had been there, it's the source of our words, which define who we are.

I tried placing both parts of the seed (Adam's part combined with mine) in my mouth to moisten it. Then I put it in the damp earth under a tree to create our offspring. The seed grew cold and shriveled up.

We made another attempt.

I tried putting the two parts of our seed between the two slates (the way I had used them to look after the fire), as if it were a dormant spark capable of blossoming into the flames of life. Our seed became stolid and lazy and shrank; when I separated the slates to take a look it was no more than a brittle scrap.

We tried our hand at creation again. I put both Adam's half and mine into a cup with some warm water. I made sure it didn't get cold. I fed it a few drops each day to keep the liquid it was sitting in fresh. I imagined that our daughter would be born with a fish's flexible tail and be able to swim the seas of the world without harm. She would belong on both water and land, the ideal home. As the days passed our seed dissolved like a lump of sugar in water.

We tried once more, one half Adam's, one half mine.

I nestled it safely in the branches of a tree like a bird's nest, ensuring it wasn't stifled. Adam and I took turns warming it with our breath, talking to it, telling it stories. Adam enjoyed this; I did not. I noticed that the tree was unaware of me. Its branches broke when I leaned on them. The seed looked exactly the same; it hadn't changed at all, as if it weren't alive. It annoyed me to see our baby grow like a stranger, a foreigner to our surroundings, and our surroundings foreign to it. I let Adam look after it, keeping it warm, and that's when I began to record our history, carving it on stone.

Using the dry thorn of a thistle, a wedge of rock, and a pile of large, smooth stones that turned a bright white color when you scraped them, I carved our descent from the Divine Mount, how we obtained fire, our stay by the river, and our subsequent journey, right up to the moment when we nestled our spawn between the branches of a blossomless tree. I thought that if we didn't record our past, engraving it on stone and making it part of our present, we wouldn't be able to get our seed to sprout.

Adam was determined to keep our cold seed warm. Up in that tree like a monkey, he told the seed a different version of our past.

As I chipped away at the stones I couldn't hear much, just snippets here and there; I thought Adam was making up stories to convince it to sprout. Mostly I ignored Adam, letting him babble on and on, without paying any attention.

"You're not getting anywhere," I'd shout up at him from time to time, trying to make him see reason. I was less concerned about his string of lies than our seed, cold as the bone of a dead buzzard. Adam didn't raise his voice, he just continued with his string of fairy tales, trying to coax and cajole our babe to life. He was lying, but how else would you turn a piece of ice into a baby?

135

When I finished recording our history on the stones, making our origins quite clear, our past written in code, I climbed the tree to take a look at the state of our seed. It looked like it had become the bark of the tree. It was nothing, not a fossil, just another bump on the branch where Adam dozed, muttering in his sleep. I shut his mouth and heard the tree say, "I'm here to remind you of the word you already know, the one that some have forgotten."

Adam mumbled away in his sleep, repeating tales he hadn't tired of telling the four winds, without my having any idea what he was saying: "I was first, and Eve came from me. They made her from one of my ribs, she's not as important, just the offshoot of a piece of me, an afterthought, worthless."

That was going too far. The tree had helped me hear the ridiculous lies my ears had been ignoring. I jumped down from the tree, infuriated. I filled our cups with fresh water. I stoked the fire. I got out the stone cooking pot, on which I had also engraved an episode from our past, true to the facts.

In the days that followed, Adam continued to insist upon his lies, repeating them over and over again—not much for talking, he had become a chatterbox who seemed not to tire of repeating the same things.

I made friends with three dogs and fed them. They were my allies.

43

More Attempts at a Child

When I stopped being angry at Adam for his stupid lies, we tried again.

I held both fertile parts of our seed in my hand, closing my fist around it tightly. I slept with my hand like that and, to help, with my jaw clenched shut as if I were dangling from a precipice, hanging on to a rope with my teeth.

Something began to stir in my fist, a butterfly fluttering its wings. I wasn't fooled. I held my fist tighter, keeping it closed, convinced it was death giving its last gasp.

I kept my fist shut. Inside, the death throes continued.

We were thirsty. We drank water. We ate raw food. I wanted to make us a stew. I felt like filling myself with something I sliced, seasoned, and cooked. But I also wanted to keep holding my fist tight to keep whatever it was from escaping, to finish cooking it. At the fireside, when I put a handful of herbs in the clay pot, I opened my fist without thinking; the undeveloped seed fell on the coals. I had made a mistake: it's impossible to cook with one hand. There's just no way. My mouth caused the death of my first potential child.

My dogs howled.

44

Further Attempts

Adam and I both tried again at the same time. First Adam put our seed inside his anus. That ended quickly; nothing came of it since the seed came back out the next time he emptied his bowels. There's a bit more to explain about the other attempt.

I placed our seed in my right ear canal. My brain and my seed sang in unison night and day. At night the bushes murmured along, each of their leaves joining in. The greenery imitated my song to the seed in a thousand tones and voices.

Our seed took root in my ear. Its branches appeared and climbed my head, its foliage growing close across my forehead and thickening.

But it was particular: if Adam desired the relief of shade, our plant-child grew away from him, in the opposite direction, refusing to provide him shade. Because of this (and other things), when I was asleep Adam came and pruned the branches of our child mercilessly, not a single leaf was left. Adam scattered salt on each stump.

Adam's work did not sit well with me. I had hoped that this child of ours would soon bear fruit, and that both it and its roots would prove delicious, perhaps as much as the original apple. The very idea disgusted Adam. *Eating our offspring! How could you think such a thing and deny what I've said about you! Despicable Eve! The very thought of consuming our offspring proves my version of our past is true.*

Several days later, I pulled out the tiny roots and shriveled trunk, the cadaver of that attempt. It was pointless and depressing to carry a dead thing around in my head.

45

The Horse Is Born unto Them

We kept on trying, though we were angry at each other. We understood that we needed to look after our seed and were united in this common cause. We needed to care for it like it was something of *ours* within my body for it to ripen to maturity.

Adam had an idea and we agreed to try it: he planted his seed in my hair. Just his part.

My scalp protested mightily against this visitor, and the commotion seemed to ferment his part of the seed. Once it started growing, my hair disobeyed orders, curling up around it. But my contribution to Adam's seed prevailed; it looked like a turban of hair winding around itself, rocking and nourishing Adam's half of the seed.

They grew in sync: hair and child. My turban became enormous. It moved, leaping elegantly.

My long, lustrous hair fell to my shoulders the first time that the little horse it was rocking kicked. Divine, blessed animal.

And that is how we conceived the horse, out of hair. Our child reminded us of our hooves, Adam's seed, my skin, my dreams, my fits of temper.

Horse of fleeting, changeable dreams. A horse is an animal that sleeps on its feet.

The horse was beautiful, but it couldn't speak, so it didn't satisfy me. Adam, on the other hand, was in a kind of paternal delirium, he was so pleased with our progeny. He could tell the horse what to do. He no longer followed me around, watching what I was doing, getting angry at me; he kept busy teaching *his* horse to do things. He even began to ride it. He was a Father, swollen with pride, arrogant, bossy.

My yearning for words grew because, with the arrival of the horse, Adam ceased to listen. The horse filled his days. But when I insisted, he came around. We would never disown our horse, how could we?

Again, we tried to make a child. I gave Adam my fertile half of the seed, spitting on it and sprinkling other things atop it while I sang. I made an incision in my belly beside my navel, and I placed our attempt to procreate there.

When it started to grow and sought more room my bowels moved around in annoyance, pushing it out of the way into the hostile atmosphere. The gelatinous fetal matter fell out, a sad imitation of a creature, lifeless.

46

Copying the Beasts,
and What Happened When We Tried

We'd have to do what the beasts did. I realized it one night in a dream.

My belly was the place the seed needed to grow. It wasn't the obvious choice, because we're not like beasts; we give birth to beings capable of language, not to creatures made in and from nature, but to descendants of that anomalous fruit (the apple), my appetite for pleasure and fire, and our own fragility. Contrary to all logic, my belly was the most likely candidate.

That's how Adam and I came to mate for the first time. Our seed began to form inside me.

I began to smell different. My shape changed: I was all belly, beautiful, big Belly. There was someone inside me, growing slowly, hearing and feeling. Which is why I smelled more things, felt more sensations—my clitoris more than it had been before—my eyes and my skin were keener, I understood more clearly. While I was growing the child, I was also growing myself into someone new and different.

My newfound state had an immediate effect: Adam felt out of place. I noticed he was frightened and angry. What was happening was so far outside his control and beyond his ken that he decided he had nothing to do with it. He wondered, *What if she's only using her seed and throwing my contribution away?* Adam told himself that our potential offspring was spending so much time inside me that it would receive all its nourishment from me and never leave my side. What about him? Who and what was he? He realized he had been supplanted. He gave up.

Adam stopped paying attention to our horse-child, which ran off to the plains, to dream alone and try to conceive another little horse.

As soon as we realized the horse had run away, Adam tried to destroy the history I had recorded on the stones, hitting them with a club and his fists. I intervened and was able to stop him, despite his fury. Ever since I had evolved into the big Belly, I had become stronger.

I wanted to lock Adam up, to keep him next to me until our child was born, but I couldn't. Adam escaped. He slept in the open air. I have no idea what he did all day long. I kept an eye out to make sure he didn't return to the place where our history was recorded, preserving memory.

And our child grew solid, like a tree, and just as soulful; a tree I had all to myself, a pink sun. I felt it move around. I spoke to it and my little one responded. My body changed further, and not just my belly. My legs seemed to change their relationship to the ground. My breasts grew. My hair became shiny and brittle. My sense of smell sharpened.

The next thing I knew Adam wanted to destroy *me*.

Adam was all worked up, eager for destruction. The speed of his movements changed. He became predatory. Every time he saw me, he attacked me. I built a fence of long canes around the entrance to our home. I let the dogs loose. They wouldn't attack Adam, but they would let me know if he was nearby.

I built another fence when I sensed the child would soon arrive.

47

Cain Arrives

I awoke in the embrace of unparalleled pleasure, pleasure greater than you'd think the senses could perceive. I knew the moment had arrived. I stayed inside our tent. The sensation washing over me was so strong that I couldn't stand. I squatted down, slick with sweat. My breathing, my muscles, everything had changed due to the bounteous pleasure that embraced me. I pushed. The child came out between my legs, covered in the sweet liquid that had been inside me. It was a delicious sense of relief, although it ended that unparalleled feeling I don't know how to describe. I gave the child a name: Cain.

Cain was tied to me by a cord, like a pup to its mother. I cut the cord and made a knot in what had connected Cain to me, like a button and a buttonhole. My body released the bag that had been holding him. I buried it at the entrance of our tent, singing to it in thanks for its service: it was the nest that had given us our child.

I considered calling to Adam to come and see him. But I was also afraid of him. I didn't have the energy to defend us. Now that I held the child in my arms, I had to protect both of us.

I slept a few hours with the child at my breast. I thought, *I must tell Adam, but in a way that he can see, and remember, and believe that the seed this child came from was ours, a two-part seed.*

48

Eve Calls to Adam

The next morning, I called Adam, shouting at the top of my lungs outside the tent. He came, looking sullen, and speaking to him was a disaster. I prefer not to remember.

Cain, who grew rapidly in the hours following his birth, paid little attention to the babble from his father's mouth; his ears didn't know hate, although understood everything. He blocked Adam's curses. While Adam was spitting out his words, Cain kept saying, "Life is good. How can you say what Eve has given us is bad?" That sentence sums up part of Cain's essence.

49

Eve Gathers the Creatures

I knew what I had to do: quickly conceive another child and make a show of fertility *outside* my body. I had to expose the activity inside me.

I went to an angel, who called a giant.

(An aside: I called the Angel using what remained of the stone that he angrily threw at me, unintentionally granting me so many riches. I picked up a piece of the angel-stone and spoke: "Stone, be mine, call upon the beautiful being who gave me fire, soul of the hearth that softens food and awakens so many flavors. Call him to me."

But the crystal didn't reply. I removed my clothes. My breasts round with milk, with life. I touched my clitoris, awakening a new sensation since the arrival of Cain. I placed the fingers of my other hand on one of my breasts, feeling something new there, too, something great.

I said, "I knew you to be beautiful from the moment I saw you, fire-bearer, you gave me the awareness of beauty. Come! Take from me. I need you.

"I summon one of the giants, too, because I know you enormous beings spy on me. You decide which one. Angel, beauty manifest in fire, keep the Giant's wickedness in check, be kind . . ."

That did it. My ritual of the flesh summoned them both.)

—

I have mentioned the role these other beings played in our early days only in passing, because our life was so incredibly full of discoveries that there was no time for them. But they were there, the fire-bearing creature of Light, the Angel, that beautiful being per se, and the oversized, fearsome beings who electrified the atmosphere with trembling and danger. Those were the giants.

The giants were a group. The Angel was always solitary. The giants knew how to laugh, their spirit was like the breath of dawn, they perpetrated monstrosities, the let themselves be trampled by the wild beasts only to tickle them to death. They looked benign but they weren't. Of course, the angels didn't even appear benign.

I needed them all for the show I was going to put on for Adam. Once they appeared I spoke to them, begging: "Giant, give me madness. Angel, give me beauty and scent, and fire."

They both desired me, each regarding me with a different kind of attraction, aroused by the idea of participating in the adventure of creation.

The giants and the angels held a conclave I didn't take part in, of which I can only imagine exclamations which don't portray them well.

As they plotted, they were thinking of Adam more than anything else.

50

Menstruation

At their conclave they decided that menstruation would be the way to show Adam that my body was generating life. Showing him what appeared to be spilled blood but wasn't.

Adam fell for it, and I went along with the plan.

But monthly menstruation wasn't the price paid, that's nothing; it was birth, because they decided to add pain to childbirth. I confirm that the giants and angels came up with this idea for the theatrical effect it would have on Adam, giving him a reason to believe he had played a part.

To keep him from feeling irrelevant, Eve would suffer through birth, making him feel privileged. He experienced no pain at all, he gave his part of the seed, and the woman contributed her pain.

What a stupid, successful conspiracy.

A bad idea, most of all. Adam, brimming with resentment, left his mark on Abel.

Meanwhile, Adam had been reinventing our history to reflect his feelings. And he decided that what you have already heard had come to pass:

51

Adam Said

Enough nonsense! Adam said that a He (whose name could not be spoken) created everything; He made it all out of clay and infused it with the breath of life so that He could enjoy creation. Because Adam was alone, He decided to make Eve from a rib.

I was nothing more than a part of an angry man.

And furthermore, Adam said, he was not just the first, and the origin of my person, but also when I ate the fruit, which was forbidden (?) by Yahweh (?), I sinned (?), which caused our expulsion (?) from Eden, which was Paradise (a fantastic lie); because of me we had to work as a punishment (outrageous), and experience the pain of childbirth (you already know the truth).

In his Cain way of speaking, every time Cain heard these Adamic ravings he said, "But Adam, knowledge is a good thing, life is good, how can you say that what Eve has given us is bad?"

52

Abel Arrives

The day to give birth arrived. It did not announce itself with pleasure, as it did with Cain. The pain hit me like a lash crisscrossing my body from my neck to my toes, from my jaw to my navel and lower still.

I had to shout, howl, roaring in a way my ears didn't recognize; I had no idea I had such a voice.

When the shouting ended: sweat and serenity. I had pushed I don't know how many times, stopped, and heard "It's a boy!" from Abel.

I didn't care. As far as I was concerned it could be a headless monster with seven legs covered in thorns like a cactus . . . I couldn't have cared less!

53

The Thing Called Abel

Abel, whom I immediately nicknamed The Whip, grew exponentially more bitter. He lived at his father's side, staying close to the sheep and especially to one bitch Adam had beaten into submission. That dog adored Abel. He was overprotected by both Adam and the dog, he followed them around night and day; a whiny crybaby, he had no idea how to be alone. His mother's strength had left him at birth.

Adam, for his part, spoke at length with his creation—his "He"—and not at all with me. He tried to order me around—but as you'll agree, that's not speaking. So I ignored him.

54

Adah Is Born

Adah was born (I called her My Delight, because that's what she was), the third I gave birth to in the manner of the animals, but born with a clitoris—wondrous, splendid surprise! That apple was truly a thing of wonder.

Adam tried to give Adah orders, which differed greatly from the ones he gave his sons. I didn't want to allow this, but I didn't have to intervene because Adah My Delight turned a deaf ear.

Adam preached that the Lord of Armies would eliminate the Kadmonites, Perizites, Kenites, Jebusites, Hittites, Ammonites, Kenizzites. A heart filled with hate makes enemies of mere shadows and sees shadows where there are none. He fell into a kind of knowledge-fog.

55

Fraternal Rivalry

In the meantime, I sowed, cultivated, and succeeded in creating a fierce rivalry between the two brothers. My garden of hate was the link between Cain-Seeds and Abel-Whip. I didn't keep the hate I had been harboring against Adam inside me; I infected them both with it, which I thought would free me from it.

Adam worked on refining his story, which he had the nerve to call "my version of events." A version born not of honest recollections, but of anger and his Adamite fog. His hate was more direct and, more worrisomely, targeted others.

56

Adam and Abel Invent Prayer, and the Slaughterhouse

Abel and Adam spoke to a "He." They made up prayers that allowed them to repeat their monologue ad nauseam. They invented rituals. Soon, Adam and Abel wanted to forbid working the land and taking pleasure in its bounty. Adam wanted only to kill. He made an arrow, wounded a young deer, and ate the whole thing, from its nose to its tail, leaving nothing behind.

That was the beginning. Abel herded up a bunch of goats, tamed them—just as his father had done with the horse—and killed them; he skinned them; he tanned their hides to make goat-skins; he hung their bodies to drain their blood and cut them into pieces—here the heads, tongues, livers, kidneys, stomachs, lungs, hearts, breasts, brains; there the legs, necks, lips, tallow.

They hung from branches, from ropes that Abel-Whip got from Cain-Seed. Great was Cain's displeasure when he learned where the ropes he wove from the plants he grew had gone. Displayed in pieces like this, the animals that had followed him obediently or that had fought against becoming his captives were all part of his dominion, and he walked among them, dressed in lambskin.

Once their blood had been let, they were eaten. He left the suckling lambs whole and roasted them. He did the same with the yearlings. And with the cattle. The smell turned my stomach.

He called himself a shepherd, omitting the obvious "butcher." He had been a shepherd before; the corral where he had kept his animals in pens, declaring they were his property—would such absurd drivel have occurred to anyone else?—so he wouldn't have to drive them elsewhere to their deaths was all his. He slit their throats in the very place where they grazed.

"My son disgusts me," I said to myself. I urged Abel to get rid of the corral and remove his garden of death from our sight, but Adam defended him, arguing that he needed to keep them close to protect them. Protect them! To kill them and rub our noses in the butchery. In the distance, at dusk the hills appeared to bleed to death from their heights, one more cadaver.

57

I Gave Birth to Two Daughters

I gave birth to a set of twins: Fire and Ice. Two pushes, two different girls: one had black, curly hair like me, and her skin was like mine: dark. The other was pale and her hair was colorless, as if my womb had only enough color for one, the firstborn, with red lips. One was irascible, unpredictable, and impassioned, while the other seemed insensate to everything, in a completely different orbit, like ice; she deliberated on every reply. The fair one slept. The black one laughed, moved around, and responded to things swiftly. They were the last ones to grow up immediately at birth; thereafter any babe born of woman would be a child for a few weeks—generations later they would be children for a whole, endless decade.

58

There Are Almonds and Then There Are Almonds

The first almonds that Cain-Seeds and I ate were, to quote him, "pathetic, Mama, they seem to be starving." It was a lot of work to pry them from their inedible shells. When toasted, they acquired a pleasant flavor and texture, but they were unfortunately small as sesame seeds, though they tasted better. By then we already knew that there was a solution to this little problem. Cain had overcome more difficult ones. He did what he had done previously; to obtain the desired size, crossed one with the other using the branches of young trees, until there were three or four different fruit trees. Eventually, one produced a treasure that we still eat today.

And apart from the almond, we found a seed that looked like the original, the one I took when we left Eden. So many attempts to, one day, finally produce a paradisiacal apple. I didn't see him do this, that comes later.

59

Glazed Pottery, Jewelry

Cain-Seeds, Adah My Delight, and I made different kinds of ceramics; improving the oven, we were able to glaze our vessels. Everything changed: stews, crops, our palates.

We made necklaces, earrings, bracelets, and clothes, because we worked hard at the loom too. We painted shapes on the clothes to match the ones on our skin.

60

Adam's Dogged Lies

Adam insisted upon his version of history, continuing to repeat his stupid lie. Why was it stupid? As if what I've already said weren't enough, here's another reason: Earth itself would have rejected Adam's confabulation because of the reductive way he told the tale, that He of the sacred powers made man out of Earth's dust, exhaling the breath of life into his nostrils, making man a living being. That simply couldn't be, and if something like that *had* occurred, it would have had more in common with other stories that tried to make sense of Adam's tale. To wit:

"When He sent the Archangel Gabriel to gather the dust that He needed to create Adam (a red handful, a copper-colored one, one white, and one black as the liquid rock from a volcano), Earth protested in both words ('I invoke Allah against you, Gabriel') and such decisive, abrupt action that Allah gave up.

"But not for long. Soon afterward He called the Archangel Michael and told him, 'Gather red, brown, white, and black dust from the four cardinal directions.' Earth protested mightily (with earthquakes and tsunamis, alternating droughts and floods, spouting lava, and spitting fire nonstop from within, blowing hurricane-strength winds, lowering the temperature until the seas froze and increasing it so suddenly that the snow turned to steam). Earth repeated: 'I invoke Allah against you, Michael.'

"Then the Creator sent the Angel of Death, who did not cease until his mission had been accomplished. Then Earth became fearful and kept her silence."

If it were true (and it definitively is not) that Adam came from a handful of dust and a breath, then the dust was delivered by the Angel of Death, and the breath was therefore one of dread and hate.

61

Earth's Strength

Not a day passed that we did not experience Earth's energy, power, and strength. We heard her voices (because she has an infinite number of them, not like that guttural one in Eden, melancholy and ghastly) creating the spectrum of life, from the buffalo to the macaw, from the wolf to the alligator, from the falcon to the manta ray to the deer, and the rainbow of fruits and vegetables. Earth protected us or treated us roughly, the same way the giant rock at the foot of the precipice would treat us (and as we know that's where we have recorded our history from the beginning, because Earth urges us to record it. Earth is the reason the first tree spoke, she is the reason we, ourselves, speak. If we were more like her, so very many things would not have transpired. For starters, we wouldn't have spent an age in lifeless Eden.)

END OF BOOK FIVE

Eve's loose papers

ANOTHER VERSION OF EVENTS, FROM AN
AUTHORIZED SOURCE:
When Earth understood that He had put Adam to sleep to make
him a fertile companion who would bear him fertile daughters,
she shook with fury. She asked Him:

"Why are you doing this? What am I going to do with so many
people living off of me!"

"What I want is for living creatures, the ones that live in the
sea, the land and the air, to witness the enormous difference
between my Being and that of the people, and for that I need
many of them."

"But think about me. I don't have the strength to produce
enough food for a pack of Adamites."

He answered:

"Don't worry, between the two of us we'll find a way to feed
the hordes."

They made an agreement: for Him, night; for Earth, day. He
would help Earth to produce enough by making the skies rain to
keep Earth damp, and during the night He would make the people
sleep so they could digest their food and recover their strength;
growing strong in the dark, humanity would populate all parts of
the Earth, growing rice in swampy regions, beans and gourds in
the earth, oysters and fish in the seas; they would harvest, reap,
fish, and hunt on land and at sea.

After reaching their agreement, both He and the Earth defined
the unforgivable exceptions to the natural order of things: any
wretch who betrayed Him or his own self would be unable to

sleep; any group that cursed, slandered, or plundered the Earth senselessly would be subjected to lethal heatwaves and freezes.

NOTE FROM EVE:
If anyone created me, it was a goddess.

If I could choose my Goddess, it would be Earth. In this scenario, Thunder abducted me and took me to Eden, making me lose my memory temporarily.

ANOTHER PAPER:
If you had been created by a goddess, Eve, it must have been the mother of Coyolxauhqui, Coatlicue. Coatlicue, the giver of all life and all death; two serpents (the kind that slither along the earth) spring from her decapitated head, and an eagle (that soars high in the sky) from her mutilated legs. She unites opposites. She is action and she is thought, the past and the present, a hybrid beyond the distinct natures combined in her one body. She is perfect in her imperfection. She, mother of us all, would have given you different instincts and she would have given them to us as well. Eve, I pray for this to the terrible mother of creation: Coatlicue.

And if this were the case, Coatlicue would rule all four cardinal points: west, north, east, and south:

You will go toward the light.

You will go toward the world where death originates.

And then you will go toward the region of the sacred fields.

And then you will go toward the region of the thorns, the south.

ANOTHER:
My daughters mated and all my children enjoyed it. The food we cooked became more and more delicious. Each season our fruits were more flavorful. We lived for pleasure. Memories grow vague

and we think that this was Eden, but it wasn't; this was Earth, a backdrop for pleasure.

ANOTHER PAPER, AN ASIDE:
(Did the delicious, original apple drive its seeds into the Earth, leaving its mark on her, too? Or was it Earth who, as the facts confirm, generated life in the tree that bore the delicious fruit when Thunder wasn't paying attention?) (Was Earth the surreptitious gardener in Eden? Did the tree accidentally grow an offshoot from its deep roots all the way up to the sandy surface of the first ridge, and from there sneaking along between earth and sand all the way to the first magical ridge, taking hold in one of its corners?) (Or is it that magnificent Earth, mother of all language, instigator of all memory, maker of life, didn't need that hesitant offshoot of the root—which made its way between the sand, the rocks, and the pieces of reddish stone from the mouth of the volcano—to transmit the life that the apple passed on to me, making us all earthly creatures?)

ONE ABOUT ADAM (AND A DAUGHTER'S REPLY):
"I was greater than the greatest ever created, and the most handsome, most perfect, because He, whose greatness makes him unnameable, made me in his image and likeness.

"It's a fact: no one was more beautiful, more capable, more agile, stronger, or wiser, because before I was born, before my soul was assigned to my body, He showed me man's fate. He gave me a companion, woman . . ."

"Woman! For god's sake, Papa! Enough!"

"I've said it once and I'll say it again, that's what we call humans *mankind*—because man came first, he was and always will be the model . . ."

"Are you saying men are superior?"

164

"No one is superior apart from Him. Though I should remind you that only I was made in his perfect image."

"Enough, Papa, enough!"

ANOTHER ABOUT ADAM:

"Eve was not first," he burst out. "I was able to love the first one, who was so beautiful, because I didn't witness her birth. Unlike the woman, the one you mistakenly call Eve; I would rather have had nothing to do with her. How could it have been any other way after I saw how she was made from a piece of my thigh? She always disgusted me."

SOMEONE ELSE'S:

Adam's hair stood on end when he bit the apple.

It was hilarious.

ONE ABOUT CAIN:

. . . if what you say about the apple is true, Adam, knowledge is a good thing, life is good. How could you say that what Eve gave us is bad?

ONE ABOUT ABEL:

. . . he made percussive instruments from the bones of the animals he killed. Drums from their skins. None of them had names, nor did Abel have any intention of creating rhythm with them, giving them purpose: he wanted to beat and dominate, to make us like the creatures he had beaten, inert bodies bellowing with fear, a symphony of noise.

Because what he was doing was terrifying.

I tried to convince Cain that he should respond in kind. He didn't listen; following his intuition, he used his reed flute, which imitated the gentle sound of the wind in the branches of trees with the giant leaves, branches that hardly ever swayed in the breeze, more solid than rigid, like stones on a precipice that know they'll never fall into the abyss.

He entranced us, making the warlike sounds calm our spirits. It didn't sound like a storm, nor was it like the loud sound that accompanies a ray of lighting that parts dark skies or splashes a pale brightness across blue ones.

We were all in a trance; Abel brooded. He knew he would confront Cain and he knew he would defeat him, bringing him back to the fire, lifeless. I don't know whether he thought of eating him, although it's possible he wanted to. Thinking it over, he realized there was a possibility he'd lose. So he hid his seed.

ANOTHER FROM ANOTHER (ALSO SUPPOSEDLY BY EVE):

I believe I knew that my body shed several daughters, grown inside me, though my muscles, bones, skin, and eyes were not completely mine yet. I never had my own birth, my own father.

They split off from me without pain, without awareness, without them (or me) even trying. Let's say it was like my hand or my nose had decided to walk off. Perhaps I was like a hydra for that period of time, but not my head—a hydra below the waist. Even though there was no pain.

ANOTHER:

Abel's portion of seed awoke.

Sneaking between the legs of Abel's sisters, it produced my grandchildren with colorless skin, almost translucent or pink—white men and women with pale hair. Next to my daughters, they looked like shadows that night might have painted, but they were empty shadows—shaped like us, but without the noticeableness of shadows. Quasi-white, but not as white as clouds.

166

ANOTHER PAPER, SUPPOSEDLY EVE'S, BUT DIFFERENT:

I developed a malady I find myself unable to explain. It didn't come on quickly but rather in a gradual way. The first symptom was slight irritation at the bright light of midday.

People, like plants, seek light, following it like faithful dogs. But I found I needed to protect myself from it. I moved the hearth inside the house, against the wishes of everyone else; they liked to stir the embers and gaze at the many hues of the fire. For me the fire was not an object of admiration, inspiring reflections, but rather a tool for changing the character of the elements, for working, for life, for transformation; for the others, the fire represented restfulness.

My aversion to light got worse. I moved the mortar and pestle under the roof where I stored our grain. If no one brought me the harvest, I ate whatever was at hand. My reaction to the light was something physical I couldn't control; it was more than a dislike, as I have described, it was a reflex. I stopped leaving the house. I closed the windows and covered them. Next, I hid the fire in a container I built out of bricks—which improved the process of cooking. Accidentally, I found something that fermented dough, making it rise, baking bread. And the same with vinegar. I was vigilant against flies. My hearing guided me in the darkness of the shadow-world I had succeeded in creating.

Even when it began to rain that wasn't enough to alleviate my allergy to light, which had become much more pronounced. I could no longer bear even the weak light of a heavily overcast day. Deeply upset by my body's reaction to light, and eager to behold the Earth, I found serenity in the idea of telling my story. I had ink and parchment in my room. I had a way to do it.

But instead, I discovered how to make bread. I fermented dough. I put it in the oven. We relished it.

One night, I realized that my two survival instincts were one and the same: making bread was making ours what fate had gifted us. Bread: history; bread: storytelling; bread: pleasure.

Without bread, without pleasure, without light, I would have died inside. But I discovered bread, and it led me to the light. And its light led me to tell this story here, among others.

THE STORY OF ONE OF EVE'S DAUGHTERS:
This is what I heard Eve say, and I'm certain that this is what she said:

1. When everything was Chaos, I wasn't there but I was part of it. Those who speak of dark monsters that made their way through wild emptiness are liars. They contend that these foul terrors drifted around in pieces, the head of one in orbit, its foot standing on another's belly, its other limbs strewn about willy-nilly. They say that each piece, separated from the whole, yearned for the others, and that the gravity that ought to have brought them together worked against them, pushing them farther and farther away from each other. They take it even further, saying it was this yearning of each body part to be united with the others that brought them together and made them one, and that thanks to the work of these terrors we have what we see today. Ridiculous! The fact is that there was no thing, no nothing, just Chaos, which contained the beginning and the End.

   Something tied up the loose ends, or undid the knot, or detangled it: the elements were established. And it didn't happen in an instant because Time didn't exist in Chaos.

2. Biting the apple and the pleasure in it led to our first act of procreation. It wasn't intentional; you were the product of pleasure; you arose from the joys of smell and taste and the residues of both of these—mostly the latter, because it has more matter, if you don't believe me just consider how you smell.

   If Adam really was made of dust, I think the dust they used was from sweet-smelling, chewed-up fruit, what's left after grinding it with your teeth, delighting in it, finding the pleasure in it, that feeling. Otherwise, I don't believe it.

   Other distantly related creatures are perhaps unaware of this feeling, the pleasure, the delight. But at least two species realized what biting that piece of fruit did, and they're like us.

   The universe of smaller creatures was invited to the table of life as we understand it, the cultivated life, the life we built for ourselves. An infinity of creatures—flying, crawling, walking, and climbing—arose from that one bite in my mouth. When they began to fly, it was not long before we knew we were their prey. When they began to crawl, they realized in the blink of an eye that our flesh—first mine, then Adam's—represented the most delicious sustenance and their own survival.

   When we rushed down from Eden, they came with us. They ran and flew alongside us. When we rested, they rested; when we started moving again, they followed us.

   I understood that it was essential to give them enough that they would leave us in peace.

3. We entered Earth surrounded by our progeny, the

insects. When we arrived, there was not a single flower in sight. We needed flowers.

4. Cave, house—roof.

5. The ferns, the reptiles, the insects, the world without flowers. Life, hidden.

6. Alas, dragonflies with serrated teeth, forming the shape of a heart when they mate to reproduce.

7. The food chain, which is to say, how we ate: first, the so-called apple, except in the garden.

8. On our way down to Earth, when the most we could do was drink water and grind ice with our teeth, we dreamed of having another bite {of the apple}. Next came salt. Protected by huge clouds of ash issuing from countless burning mountains, which constantly filled the sky as we descended alongside the river, we delighted in tasting mollusks, some of which were softened and changed by lively flavors when we put them in our fire. Then we tried oysters, and in the first lake we discovered other things, including a variety of clams, orange mussels, and white scallops stuck to their shells, extracted with the slate that, like fire, was my constant companion.

    When we arrived at the edge of the sea, we ate octopus and squid. The waves of the unpredictable tides, the majority of which were caused by constant earthquakes, and the rain of fire from the volcanoes caused us to take refuge until one day it was no longer possible for us to go out. The cave we had been sheltering in, made of limestone and salt, became so hot we were forced to explore its depths. We went down a series of dark passages, reluctantly and blindly for the most part, trying to find respite from that infernal heat, which was burning and painful on our skin, and where we wouldn't feel like we were suffocating. There was no food, so we had to eat our progeny, the small insects.

Because the creatures we begat in the original garden had been small, tiny, but on Earth they were enormous. Pollen abounded—the flowerless plants in this world needed absurd amounts of pollen to reproduce. These enormous insects ate their own kind, regardless of what species they were.

Earth was home to cannibals, many of them low creatures. The ones that came along with us had also been affected by the pollen and the influence of the giants. Many lost their wings. During the time I'm telling you about, most of them were our companions, dragging themselves through that subterranean labyrinth with us.

We made a fire with my stones, taking care to build it where there was a place for the smoke to escape and for fresh air to enter. And so, below the surface, we devoured our progeny after salting and roasting them; they didn't taste anything like the delicious apple or the tender clams, they gave us pleasure and sated us, accompanying our confinement with their flavors.

When Adam and I were poking around in passageways that had probably been created by some of the arthropods or arachnids we had seen on our journey, we discovered a small grotto that was so black it appeared to shine. Its walls were soft, almost caressing us.

Earth continued to shake constantly, letting us know that deep as we were, we were still on its territory, that it commanded the ocean and ruled its bowels as well. Because of the shaking, the tunnels were constantly changing, and they led us to a passage where a reddish shaft of light fell from the highest point of the cavern, which was open to the surface. Fire began to drip from the hole, liquid fire that sprinkled down in sparks of different sizes. It didn't last.

The light in the cavern was tinted red. It illuminated an odd-shaped pond, which had some reddish rocks jutting out of it. The water was translucent, with agile blue fish swimming near its surface. A few had been partially toasted by the fire and had floated to the top. I took them out of the water and laid them on a colorless gray rock. In the red light they were iridescent, with a variety of colors on their scales where they had not been burned and blackened.

I salted them.

We tasted them; Adam pricked his tongue with their needle-like bones, otherwise they were soft and exquisite in both taste and texture.

On the red walls of the grotto, using the point of my slate, I celebrated our visit by depicting how it had rained fire in the cave, how the mountain had cooked (with its own fire) the delectable meat of the blue fish, and how Adam, in his haste, had been wounded. The markings on the stone, which were the color of sand and couldn't be erased by wind or water, were submerged because it began to rain insistent, fat drops, the pond began to rise, and beneath the transparent water they appeared to be magnified, fabulous, watching us.

I drew them to remember them, but it was they who held us in their memories, undaunted.

The fat drops of rain fell constantly. With the rains came the frogs, croaking monotonously to herald the night, without any imagination. There's no question that frogs don't dream, differentiating them from so many other animals.

I had to use both hands to pick up a single frog; I threw it on the fire and roasted it. To be clear: I had it in my hands because I had hunted it. That's what memory is for: I copied what I had seen the dragonflies do. First, I sat still on a rock at the edge of the water, premeditating, calculating—an acquired strategy of speed and timing. But unlike the dragonfly, I roasted my prey on the fire to share it with Adam and ate it unhurriedly, a pleasurable surprise in each mouthful.

Because frogs, with their pitiable appearance and name, get their flavor from the water, the sand, the earth, the plants, the trees, the fish, and the sounds of each passing step, of every creature that nears the pond or the stream that carries them away.

Our salt supply dwindles. Adam goes out one day, returning with a blank look on his face, looking lost, unable to express an emotion he didn't understand. He says he has just seen, for the first time, what we today call a "flower," specifically a magnolia. He describes it, his words tumbling out. I don't believe him.

At dusk, I take the same underground path he took. No sooner have I poked my head out, just my head, than my nose perceives the most colossal of magnolia trees. I wait until dark. Then I carefully come outside. I climb the tree. I shake a branch, the thinnest one I can reach. A flower falls off. I climb down and gather the fallen petals. Steps away, an almost whole flower lies, alone, wounded. I pick it up.

I hear roaring at my back; I sense the steps of a large saurian approaching. Half blind, it crushes everything in its path: the fern trees, the palms. I realize it is being guided by its sense of smell, and there is no doubt it has smelled me, if not the petals of the flower and it is pistil, all the parts of that heavily scented magnolia.

Without moving, I wait until the colossal, four-legged saurian reptile slips away, its tail zigzagging as it moves off. I repeat: it is blind, defenseless.

In the sky, clouds of ash. It's painful to breathe. I fondly recall the stuffy air of the cavern.

The earth shook, demolishing the grotto. We tried to return to the place where the dust was soft, like coal, but that passage had also been destroyed. We left via a narrow passage which had also crumbled. The light was blinding.

We rushed to find a hiding place.

What we ate along the way: mushrooms and green leaves. Bears, deer, eggs, and various kinds of marrow.

9. The bees were there.

Cain was the one who was in charge of the bees. Many years later, when a messenger delivered the news that he had founded a city in his exile and described what it was like, I understood that he had known his destiny since he was a child. Anyway, he was in charge of them, and they guided him, too.

Abel brought the pirate bees, which stole our bees' honey.

10. It became dangerous to move about underground.

When we arrived on the surface, we looked for shelter.

This is in the times before the oceans carved up the bodies of land, which today we call continents. Oversized ferns, like monstrous kapok trees, covered expanses, and beneath their green crests, ravenous creatures with two legs and voluminous tails stuffed themselves night and day, their immense jaws crushing the humongous leaves of these colossal plants. Enormous, iridescent dragonflies and some of the big predators that had succeeded in escaping the surface of the Earth, their hind legs grown long from the constant drag of the wind (the pterosaurs) flew through the skies.

There was not a single flower on all of Earth. It yearned for something beautiful.

In response to this desire, and to aid the pterosaurs in their flight, the feather came into being. I watched it sprout from the skin of a flying animal. Its beauty was necessary, but its passport to existence was its mechanical usefulness. Is flying without flying, flying? Is it possible for a clumsy body to gallop through the skies without somehow revealing the merry usefulness of its bones? Feathers were what was missing for life to continue on its way, painlessly and even happily.

Though it seemed unnecessary, this blinking of

thin filaments that is a feather, there and not there, their uniqueness, gave some meaning to the absurdity of the world.

The first feather was born at night. Every day the light was becoming more unbearable for me. We spent sleepless nights hiding in our shelters. We were so much smaller than the ravenous beings on the Earth and in the air. The jagged teeth of the dragonflies were as much a threat as the reptiles' lashing tails and cavernous mouths that could swallow us whole, leading to . . . I traveled through one of them, and survived . . .

Alas, the things I saw!

Adam's first ejaculation made him mortal.

11. Bread and our use of milk and animal fat changed my body. I had been more like a dragonfly, but now I was more like a cow.

This weight had the effect you'd expect. I walked more slowly. My hair changed, too, it became heavier. I hadn't weighed so much even when I was carrying the twins.

Because one day I had another set of twins, I called one Gog and the other Magog. My mistake was giving them those names.

ANOTHER ENTRY, SUPPOSEDLY OF EVE'S, BUT VERY DIFFERENT:

Then I prepared to mate with Angels.

Our progeny would be fleshless creatures, different from my other children in that regard. The chosen ones would know how to speak. The rest would have fire, air, light, swords and arrows, anger, and arrogance and beauty, despite their lack of flesh and bones, because their imaginary bodies would materialize once in a while, similar to a human's, but with important differences such as: weightlessness, greater strength than even the beasts, no internal organs, eyelids, or sensitive parts of their skin (their mouths were sealed since they couldn't speak whether they had lips or not, and their tongues were as dry as their fingers, which didn't have fingernails—nor did their tongues).

Since they didn't have internal organs, their immaterial bodies didn't have organs for pleasure either, since those organs were born from the inside out. There would be no distinction between male and female angels.

The majority would be whole-bodied and fully clothed, except the ones that are just heads with a neck and shoulder blades with wings attached, which take the place of arms and legs, in a way; these, the so-called cherubim, would have no clothes.

Only some of the whole-bodied ones would know how to wield a sword; for the rest who held one it was purely decorative.

BOOK SIX

62

Adah's Story

Midday. The hard, vertical light of the Sun's rays was relentless. Unusually, it had started beating down early in the morning and didn't let up, ferocious, voracious, until the afternoon had begun. Exposed to its abject cruelty for hours, we scattered without thinking, as if its unmoving brightness made us hide from our mates.

We had visions of unthinkable things. On the white rock I painted a headless animal devouring a woman, eating with her gaping neck (her thorax's fantastic mouth). I traced a herd of giraffes fleeing the ravenous animal, and two fallen palm trees; the Sun had vanquished them, too.

The first, abrupt signs of the light fading were disconcerting; though it was to be expected and we desired it, it seemed unexpected in contrast with the solidity of the midday brilliance which had seemed eternal and had enjoyed beating down on us at our expense.

Exhausted, we were also fizzing with energy—so much light! The capriciously slow pace of time, which seemed to have stopped, but suddenly began to move, plus our former seclusion and the ideas it had given us, unleashed everyone's anxieties. Overcome with emotion, we were all on edge, orphanlike.

In fact, we were orphans; I, Adah's mother, am an orphan; her father is an orphan (though he frequently mentioned his divine origins). What else could have been expected of our clan?

Exhausted, anxious, hungry, and thirsty, we gathered around the fire where the cooking pot murmured—my three daughters, Adam, Abel, our pets (which numbered nearly a dozen), and a few steps away, scores of animals that lived in captivity with Abel; he had tamed them (with his whip), they were under his command.

Beasts that lowed their master's name. The cows: "A-bel." The sheep and goats: "A-Beeeel." Each species opening their throats and bleating in praise of their master, owner, oppressor; enslaved creatures yearning for the touch of their tyrant, their provider, their savior, and their executioner. Abel never hid the fact that he was their butcher.

Abel, the (sinister) light of their eyes, had long since established the slaughterhouse as provisioner of the household; animal blood had its influence on the table, our palates, my pots, our tongues, our taste. Abel had started it and Adam supported it; I gave in, I used Abel's knife and I carved a runnel for the ingredients of my dishes into the hardest of stone.

With Cain I shared a pitchfork, a spade, the palms of our hands—he cared for his crops, just as I labored over my dishes, the dough, the vegetables. With Abel, blows and incisions became part of preparing our food, too. With Cain, it was shaping, sowing, effecting change. With Abel, it was attacking. I was the seed from which they both sprang, despite their differences. The seed had grown in my oven and at the table where I prepared our meals.

We were all gathered together, except Cain. Usually, he was the first to arrive, his arms full of things for the cooking pot—delicious blossoms, fruits, seeds, or grains, sometimes already milled.

Cain was the first to leave that morning, before (long before) there was any sign of the unusual brightness of that day. He went to work earlier than Abel did to milk his goats, as always.

Cain, by the way, was the only one who still refrained from

eating meat. "Like consumes like. And when like consumes like, it goes both ways; sister will consume sister and brother will consume father."

He said it like a sage, certain that eating sheep, cattle, and birds would turn us into assassins of our own kind. Sometimes he went even further, asserting that it was wrong to devour any creatures that had two eyes, like us. Which reminds me: he found goat's milk equally repulsive. "It's a thief's meal, you're stealing from the mother what's intended for her offspring."

And so, at the end of that infernal day, Cain was the last to arrive. He was carrying a pale wooden wheel. He showed it to us, his pride evident in his words, knowing that he had done something unique, special.

"It's a sky wheel. I made it. Out of pieces of polished hardwood which I bent here . . ."

I went over to touch his invention. The handsome object was edged with wood that really was curved, assembled carefully to make an unbroken circle. I finished my inspection without a word; I didn't need to say anything, I was filled with admiration for both the object and the deed.

Abel was the first to speak.

"Sky wheel?" he asked sarcastically.

Shifting the wheel to his left hand, Cain extended his right hand, raising his index figure to the horizon, and, turning on one foot, pointed to the circle the horizon made.

"That circle. With it . . ."

"The sky doesn't have one circle, it has many," Abel interrupted. "What you see deceives your eyes. You have to look beyond first impressions. There are at least seven circles in the blue heavens. The Creator is in the first . . . Your wheel is wrong, it violates the Creator's power."

Cain's features clouded over. He put his wheel down, leaning it against the wall.

Adah interrupted, "Abel, it's dangerous to study the universe. Forget about that, or else you'll lose your senses and you'll be sure to fall upon misfortune and take us all down with you. Don't say foolish things; trust what your eyes see."

"Adah, I know how many circles there are in the heavens, which one the fallen angels inhabit, how Earth is suspended and spins. He whispered it to me, the greatest One of all . . .

Cain's expression hardened into anger. Adah noticed, and without taking her eyes off Cain, she said to Abel, "You don't know anything. What you can't see with your eyes . . ."

"Don't be idiotic. If that were the case, we wouldn't be able to breathe, because we breathe what we can't see, but it keeps us alive, and the Spirit is in it and . . ."

"If your eyes don't know how to see what's in front of them, not even the air, you must have a pea brain."

It wasn't the first time that an argument between Adah and Abel became heated. They both broke into verbal tirades. Abel insulted her. Adah retaliated with a bone that still had meat on it, which I had set aside to flavor the stew. Adah and Abel came to blows.

Cain separated them. Abel pounced on Cain, grabbing the wheel and hitting him with it. Adah snatched the wheel from Abel, tossing it out of his reach. The beautiful thing bounced as it landed and began to roll, to the delight and surprise of my two youngest daughters, who followed it out of the room. I was the only one who noticed that we all stopped when the wheel bounced.

Cain grabbed Abel with both arms. With all my might, I yanked Cain's right arm, separating them. Abel looked at me, furious. I didn't step back. Still holding Cain by the arm, I walked straight out of the room. We left the others behind.

We passed the mangers beside Abel's pen, moving into the

darkness of night. We came to Cain's fields, which had yet to produce crops at that time of year. The land was carefully groomed, orderly, cosseted, Cain tended to it regularly, watering it and fertilizing it; healthy, fertile land lying fallow.

The Moon illuminated its furrows, casting a blue tint over them. They radiated a serenity, a peaceful light so unlike the hostile light that had hammered down on us throughout the day.

We walked. On both edges of the stream, the grass, which Cain had patiently cultivated, danced in the water's path; the stream played with the moonlight, sprinkling silvery white glimmers on the grass.

We stopped.

The frogs croaked in unison. Sparks of liquid light traced two lines dancing along the edge of the water. The frogs' throats raised their voices. Their song was yellow, more deceptive than the soft, serious light on the fields, more opaque than the sparks on the water. Some beast on the other side of the stream bellowed; its mate roared back. It was a mating call. We heard their bodies trampling the brush as they moved. Then, silence. The frogs ceased. The sparks dancing on the freezing water stopped, the creek became a cloudy stain, merging with the land. Silence.

Something hit both Cain and me. Not a physical object, but something that hurt just as much, on my skin, in my body, and even deeper than that. Cain, who was downcast, suddenly raised both his arms and burst into tears. I put my arm around him, trying to console him; I was crying, too, desolate. We realized that something was happening that was making us cry.

When the Moon came out the frogs began to croak again. They stopped. The crickets chirped, trying to assuage our grief and confusion. The Moon went behind a veil, as if the knife of our grief had stopped the clouds, impaling them upon her.

The snake, which always slept at night, slithered its large

body, hissing; the threat of its reptilian poison imposed silence and stillness.

The stream was black, the grass an invisible funeral procession.

Although we weren't present to witness what was happening where I prepared our meals, we didn't need to be, we cried as those events were taking place.

How long did Cain and I stand there like statues at the edge of the stream, aware of what our eyes could not see: what was happening beside the fireplace? Although it was beyond our field of vision, we saw without our pupils; our hands could not touch it, but we could feel it. We were in the collective conscious, in an abysmal dimension whose light revealed the pain that wounded us from afar.

In silence Cain and I turned around and retraced our steps— and that was the only sound in the dark, endless night. Our path seemed as long as that interminable day. We returned without speaking a word, each step separating us farther from one another.

Seconds before we arrived, Cain let go of my hand.

In the house an ominous silence had settled, the kind caused by the snake. Out of habit I went to stir the coals and feed the fire. As always, I turned to look for the bread dough, which was always next to the water jug. It wasn't there. The jug sat filled with water. I looked around the table for the dough. The kitchen shone like a field after battle.

63

Cain and I See What We Didn't See

Here I'll tell the story of what Cain and I felt was happening in our absence. I'll sketch it briefly, since we weren't there, and I normally write only about my own experience:

When we left, tempers calmed. They waited for our return to sit down and eat.

The two youngest sisters were playing with the wheel, trying to figure out how to make it turn upright, on its edges. One of them tried to keep it next to her as she walked, pushing it along with her palm. Following the wheel, they headed in the opposite direction from us. They were laughing, the earlier quarrel already forgotten.

Adam wasn't there, I don't know where he had gone.

Only Abel and Adah remained in the kitchen, sitting there like two lumps; then Adah went over to the dough to start kneading it again. Then Abel jumped behind her, pinning her arms behind her back, squeezing her. Lasciviously?

The dough fell to the floor. Adah freed herself from his hostile grip and defended herself against Abel. She scratched, she hit. Abel caught her from behind again. Adah hit him on the head, freeing herself once more; she picked up a pot and threw it at him, then a plate, then a cup, the pieces of broken pottery crunching beneath their feet. Abel hit Adah with a cooking pot, breaking it on her head. Attacking each other, they didn't notice they were trampling the sacred dough. Abel grabbed the knife he had carved out of bone, his contribution to the kitchen. He approached Adah, threatening her with its tip. Adah reached behind her for the jug and smashed it on Abel's forehead. Without releasing his grip on the knife, Abel lunged at Adah, pulling her down by her hair while she scratched him and hit him; Abel held the tip of his weapon against Adah's throat, pushing her into the bits of pottery and the muddied dough. He forced his thing into her violently, penetrating her, hurting her.

Adam walked in when this was happening, when the knife was still at her throat, when Abel was mounting Adah like an animal, while Adah dug her nails into Abel's back, clawing at him.

Adam shouted, "Abel, what are you doing?"

Abel removed the knife from Adah's throat. He let Adah go. Half naked on the floor, his thing standing erect, he rolled over onto his back to look at Adam.

"It's not my fault; this part of my body acted of its own accord."

Adam shrugged his shoulders; he didn't help Adah up from the floor. Adah sat up, wounded, cuts on her back from the shards of pottery, her nails broken, her face beaten, and roared at Adam, "And you made that thing! I know it and you know it too, Adam. *This* is your doing. And because you have one Abel has one, too, and he hurt me with *it*; he put it in me against my will, making a wound that can't be healed."

Adah began to cry, still as a rock that water bubbles forth from, making no sound.

Adam became angry.

Abel got up and kicked at Adah.

Adah threw a wooden bowl, which was within her reach, at him. Adam bent down, grabbing her by the head.

And so, it continued, Adam and Abel against Adah, wounding her there, where she was meant to feel pleasure; there, with their own things, and with other things, too. This was the horror that Cain and I felt from afar, sensing the terror and the pain of this scene.

Adam and Abel left, and Adah dragged herself (she was unable to walk) to her bed.

64

The Splinter of Bone

I stirred the coals in the oven once again. The dough trampled on the floor, stretched out in strange shapes, looked like it was beyond saving. Patiently, I took great pains to gather the bits that were salvageable and put them in a deep dish. I washed the dough to remove the things that had stuck to it on the ground.

In the dough I found a long splinter of the bone I had been saving for the stew, sharp and thin, longer than my middle finger. I looked at it and the splinter spoke to me.

"Adah threw the bone at Abel and broke it. Adah saw me lying on the floor and didn't pick me up, she left me there like I was useless, while the whole scene took place right in front of me . . . If she had picked me up, if she had used me, this would never have come to pass, Adah would have been able to defend herself with me. I was her weapon. It was war, it was war! It's war, Eve, war between men and women!"

I barely managed to say, "Shut up, stupid splinter! I have enough to deal with, without your complaints." I set the speaking splinter aside. I dried the dough. I sprinkled it with a little water from the jug I kept under the table, I needed to refill it and replace the jug. I added flour and water to what remained of the dough, kneading it. It still showed traces of dirt from the floor. I carefully placed it in a bowl; I added water.

The splinter didn't want to shut up.

"I'm warning you, Eve. It's one thing for Adah not to use

me, to leave me lying there like garbage, a mere witness, when I was the one who could have saved her, that's one thing. But it's another altogether for you to call me stupid, to ignore me. I've had it! From now on I will be the voice of anger and resentment."

"Damn splinter!" I muttered. "Shut up!"

"I will never shut up, ever! I will speak Abel's truth; I will be his apostle and his voice. So that no one forgets it. Because Adah didn't take me in her hands to defend herself, you shall be left without a voice."

The clouds obscured the Moon. I felt as if a cold hand had covered my eyes.

I left things just as they were—the water in the deep plate with the dough, all that remained of the chaos created by the violence between my children and Adam's fury. I found it hard to move because of the weight on my chest and my thighs. I went to lie down. I fell into an unusually heavy sleep, a sleep without dreams, perfectly still, like the cadaver of an animal.

65

The Next Morning

I awoke to hear Abel whistling happily as dawn broke in the morning sky. I stood up; as usual, he was off to do the milking, he looked peaceful, content. He wasn't the least bit angry anymore—I remember thinking, *Will anything ever have an impact on that poorly fired vessel?* He was impervious to fear because he was all Adam's anger and resentment, you should have heard him curse. Had he ever seen anything like what the splinter had witnessed after breaking off the bone, anything that had poisoned him like this? Alas! He hadn't needed to see anything. The story had turned the dog into a wolf, and that made sense because we are words, more than anything else. The trees that had refused me with words had given me more than the one that gifted me the apple, though that crunching was a way of speaking, too, an earlier way, but it was a word . . .

I went to the oven to light it and bake the bread. The water in which I had abandoned the dough the night before because I was so upset had made bubbles. I didn't move it, I just smelled it; it gave off an interesting new scent that was even more pleasing to my lungs than to my nose.

After fetching water to refill the jug and stopping by Adah to leave her a cup (I only saw her back, she was still sleeping), I removed the dough from the water and dried it. I took a small piece of the mother dough—for the next loaf of bread, and the next and the next—and tore off one more piece which I put back in the bubbly water. I kept that bubbly water with its pinch of dough in a jug whose mouth was too narrow to use for pouring and left it there.

I stirred the embers in the oven and covered it again to make it hotter.

I kneaded the bread; misused as it had been (the trampling, my forgetting it in the water), it was falling apart. I did everything I could to make it round. It didn't stay. I added a bird's egg and a little salt. I divided it into three parts with the help of some very fine cloth and braided the pieces together to give them shape. It didn't look bad, but I doubted it would rise or bake properly.

The eggs (from turtles, crocodiles, the largest from the long-legged birds that Abel kept) looked like they had survived the previous day's battle intact, but at the bottom of the pile a few that had broken in the commotion were oozing. I gathered what I could from the broken ones. The sad plait of bread looked so unusual that I used my fingertips to glaze it with what I had saved of the broken eggs. This shine made it look a little more normal. For a moment I thought I had saved our daily bread.

I placed it in the oven.

I didn't want to think about the violence between my children or let it mar the new day; I set to eliminating all traces of it. I gathered the broken shards and piled them next to the vegetables. I cleaned the wooden bowls, all of which were intact; I rinsed the cheese.

The cherries were on the floor; some of the crushed ones were still releasing their scent. I washed them and added them to the bubbly water where the dough had spent the night. I covered the container so the flies wouldn't be able to visit and fill it with their eggs.

The house had remained silent except for the sounds of footsteps and our morning routines. I continued erasing the evidence that remained of the previous night's battle royal without thinking, without feeling anything but a longing to return everything to a state of order.

I uncovered the container and added a couple of fruit peels I had left out to dry several days earlier and a handful of seeds that had been crushed in the brawl. Then I covered it again.

The bread was ready: it tasted different from our usual bread. It was the bread of grief.

Abel returned with the jug full of warm milk. He still had traces of it around his mouth. He was every inch my butcher son, the "me first" among us.

Adam smelled the milk and the bread and came to eat and drink without saying a word. Our two youngest daughters appeared to do the same, also in silence. No one said a thing about the bread tasting different or anything about the previous evening, as though my putting everything back in order had convinced them that nothing whatsoever had happened.

I didn't have any milk. I didn't raise my eyes to look at repugnant Abel: looking at him again would have made my breasts hurt where my own milk had gushed to nourish his cruel snout. My remorseful breasts.

Having consumed the milk, his mouth still full of bread, Adam broke the silence. He told us that we had fire because of him, that when he had asked God how to make it, the Creator gave him two stones and told him to knock them together. And that when he did so they birthed the first spark, which created the first flame. An utter falsehood! I didn't refute it. I kept my silence.

He said I was not the first woman. That there was another before me, whom he witnessed being created, also made from a part of his body. And that because he saw how the Maker created her, he turned away from her, and the Creator had to dispose of her because she repulsed him. That, too, is untrue. I kept my silence.

Then he said, "When the women aren't around, I'll tell you about Lilith. Oh yes, oh yes, oh yes, yes! She was the first woman. She was created the same way I was, but instead of pure dust she was made from sediment and dirt. Dirty and beautiful, divine Lilith!

He continued blathering, boasting that he was the most beautiful being ever created, the greatest, perfection itself.

I didn't open my mouth.

That's when he came out with a new story about my own origin. "At the base of my spine, where the vertebrae end, I once had a stinger. This stinger was lethal, and I could protect myself from any beast or enemy with it. One day when I was sleeping, the Creator cut my stinger off, and made Eve from it. That's the source of the poison in all her actions . . ."

Adam paused and then continued.

"And so, Cain arrived! Is it right that the eldest always arrives last?"

Cain was a shadow of himself. A trampled shadow like the bread itself, the wounded dough.

Then Adam began to speechify that the males should all make an offering to Him, the unnameable, to ask forgiveness for Eve's sins. I hadn't been expecting the bit about *my* sins, just the bit about "sins." All I said was, "Adam, for once do something sensible, just ask Abel to leave. He's the only one on this Earth who ought to ask forgiveness, and not from the one you call the unnameable, but rather from the rest of us. Give your speech to him."

Adam ignored my reply. He didn't even turn to look at me. He did the opposite, ordering Cain in particular to make an offering. His two male children were to make an offering to the unnameable Him.

195

"Women need not participate. Who would want anything from them? It's their mother's fault that we've fallen into this life of pain and suffering."

Again, I refrained from responding. But I got up from the table. I couldn't take any more. I went to see Adah, putting herb poultices on her, holding the anger and the grief deep inside me. One thought reverberated inside me: *I should never have given birth to Abel!*

66

The Offerings of Cain (the Tiller of the Soil) and of Abel (Shepherd)

You know this story: to prepare their offering Abel slit the throat of a goat from his flock, drank a mouthful of the stream that burst forth from its neck like a fountain, and quickly covered the vein so the animal's flesh would retain the blood; he picked up a pile of entrails, meat, and abundant fat from his most recent victim; he separated the bones and set the head and skin aside; as was his custom, after flaying the body he sprinkled it with salt and urine and hung it to dry on some poles a few feet away. He hung the skull of the goat from a string of dried intestine tied to a taller pole, where it shared the honor with other animal skulls—the clean ones observed the scene with their empty eye sockets, the ones that continued to rot were surrounded by flies and covered in white maggots.

The proof of his labors lay next to the pile of animal remains (Abel's offering): the knife (both sides of the blade dripped with the animals' blood from slicing their flesh away), the offal, and the blood and other bits and pieces the earth had not absorbed, and the bones torn from the flesh, ready for use, piled in a heap.

Cain carefully arranged fragrant flowers, sweet herbs, and the sprigs of aromatic trees on a small table made from slabs of rock and round stones; he sprinkled them with shavings from the trunk of a cherry tree, which were still damp, so that when he set it afire the smoke from all the different plants would emit their distinct aromas.

Once the offerings were ready Adam gave the order to light the fires.

Abel's offering produced dense, compact smoke which rose into the sky.

The scent of Cain's, a perfumed cloud, spread quickly (so quickly it looked like it was running), light and joyful, reaching almost as far as the sown fields, blessing our senses and our spirits. You could hardly tell its scented freshness apart from the pure air.

Abel's greasy fire and viscous smoke rebelled and kept its distance from our surroundings, impenetrable; when the blood burned it thickened the smoke, making us all cough and our eyes sting.

Adam didn't hesitate; coughing and clearing his throat in the Abel-ized smoke, he decreed, "Abel, your offering is good! Its smoke . . . so dense! Substantial! Like ink! Remarkable!"

He stepped away from the offering and coughed deeply. He wiped the tears and snot from his face. "I congratulate you, Abel, your sacrifice has weight and substance. You can be sure that He, the divine one, is well pleased. Abel, there's no doubt that He accepts your sacrifice! You have understood His desire for oblation and what His divine being requires.

"But yours, Cain, you must be fooling. Are you not ashamed? All you offered on your fire was grass, nothing living, nothing that would remotely please the one you have no right to name. Have you no respect? He despises your offering; He rejects it; you have not fed your fire with spirit, nor have you offered anything that lows, barks, roars, moves, flies—nothing that doesn't have roots. You offered silence, and He responds with silence. No, no, no, Cain! You have made no sacrifice; you haven't given anything up. Yours is sheer hypocrisy.

"That's why your offering, Cain, doesn't rise to the celestial abode, that's why it has been rejected."

Abel began to laugh, swollen with pride and self-satisfaction.

"Yes, I'm laughing at you! You can't get your smoke to rise, or anything else! You have a pitiful penis! It's pathetic! Even if Adah sucked you, she couldn't fuck you. Adah will suck me and fuck me!"

Cain went wild.

"Shut up! Shut up! Don't say her name!"

Adam provoked him further.

"She'll suck mine, Adah will suck *me*!"

Abel pushed Cain, taking him by surprise, and he fell. Abel and Adam pointed at him on the ground and continued mocking him.

"You only do women's work!"

"Girly-Cain the Seed-Sower!"

"Your penis is girly! Your penis is a cock-ette!"

"You've got a girly cock-ette!"

Rising from the earth in fury, Cain threatened Abel with his right fist.

"Shut your mouth or I'll get you with this!"

"Go ahead! Fuck me if you can, I'm not Adah!"

Cain didn't reply. He turned his back and as Abel continued taunting him ("Exactly like Adah! You really are a girl!") he grabbed the skull, which had dried in the sun, holding it tightly by the jaw, and shook it at Abel, who said, "I ate your Adah's cunt! Hear that? Cunt! Cunt!"

Cain raised his arm, jumped, and struck a blow at Abel with the jawbone. It knocked him to the ground, breaking his neck.

If Adam was correct, the stench had pleased this divine Him, whereas He had rejected the perfume of the dried flowers, seeds, ripe fruits, and herbs, all covered in the damp shavings from the cherry tree.

In which case, what a strange character this divinity was, to prefer the stink of unbreathable smoke to those scents that lift the soul!

Whether Adam had been right or not, Earth witnessed common sense depart for other lands that day. She knew, well before I did, that we would all wander from then on, and that my children's children would be brutes. She had done well to fear us.

END OF BOOK SIX

Loose pages, including the story of Lilith

ADAM SAYS:

Lilith and I never got along. She was trash; I was pure. She argued about everything. She told me, "Why do I have to lie beneath you like your mattress? You forget that we're equals. I'm made of dust and the breath of God, just like you. You want me underneath you to make me feel like a piece of stone that's there for your pleasure, not like a woman. No! I refuse! I won't be on the bottom. Either I do the screwing or there won't be any."

One night, the sow finally made me lose my patience. I forced her into the position I wanted. As I was about to penetrate her, Lilith, who was furious, pronounced the secret word for calling the one who created us all, rose into the air, and left me forever.

I prayed, informing the great Creator of my companion's escape. He listened, as he always does to souls who are pure. He sent Senoy, Sansenoy, and Semangelof to bring her back to me. The three angels searched high and low until they found her. I should have known from the start that she had reunited with the pack of wanton demons that lives at the edge of the Red Sea. What was she doing, if not enjoying their filth? There she gave birth to the revolting Lilim, a sizable number of them, more than one hundred Lilim per day.

"I have no desire to return to that man, he beat me whenever he liked, he wants to force me to have sex however he wants, without giving me any pleasure; he just wants to feel good without giving anything in return."

The three angels answered in unison, "Cursed Lilith, follow

our orders. Return immediately to Adam. We won't tell him what you were doing here with these disgusting demons. We won't tell him you've populated the shores of the Red Sea with all these creatures you birthed, the filthy Lilim. We'll let you return to your honest life, as honest as your life could ever be."

The Angel Senoy looked her in the eyes. "Listen, Lilith, Adam does you a great favor by lying atop you, preventing you from falling into the filth of carnal desire. No female ought to feel pleasure, because none of you are capable of restraint. And you least of all women born or yet to be born, Lilith. If you feel pleasure, the filth of which you're made will never change. Restrain yourself, obey your lord and master, and dedicate yourself to giving him pleasure, which is your lot, and what you know best. Try."

Although the reasons were irrefutable, Lilith refused to return to me. She was happy giving birth to all those mucky brats (and the Lilim, which were even worse), while the demons tempted her and gave her so much pleasure—none of them forced themselves on top of her when they screwed; they ruled their commune with a general disdain for man's inhumane and alien ways of orderliness and cleanliness (tools for the subjection of women and slaves), which didn't hold the least attraction for them.

Her Lilim lacked supervision and grew wild. They fed on bits of roots, vegetables, fruits, flowers, and herbs cooked on the fire, delighting in their delicious flavors; they had that much in common with us: they liked to enjoy their meals.

Sansenoy, the second angel, tried to persuade her. "Lilith, look at the sty you're living in. Does it not disgust you? Or at the very least cause you shame? Remember the lovely garden where He gave you a home. Return, or you shall die."

Lilith laughed at this ridiculous threat. She had left the Garden before our fall, which entailed a condemnation to death—the Fall, for which I and all my descendants can thank the iniquity of Eve, by the way, another dirty sow. It's her fault we all die. And that idiot Eve calls herself "the giver of life"! You'd have to be Eve to be that shameless.

No one knows what the third angel said to Lilith, because he took her aside to try to convince her. It's thought that she seduced him, making him fall into iniquity, because we haven't heard anything about Semangelof ever since.

Despite all these attempts at reasonable persuasion, Lilith did not return to me, nor did she die. He (the Creator, the unnameable) imposed a mighty punishment upon her: each day he killed a hundred Lilim, until not one of them was left. Thus, there's no need to fear them any longer (because each Lilim was like two Liliths).

ANOTHER VERSION, AS IF TOLD TO CAIN (WHOSE COULD IT BE?):

Generations came before you, Cain; you're not my first brother, nor are you Eve's first child.

Long ago, even before the horse, there were others. Eve systematically erased them from history. When I objected, she replied, "It's bad enough for them to accuse me of making up the story about the horse, that's why I don't say a word about anything that came before." Eve doesn't make things up, that's why she takes care to ensure nothing untrue is attributed to her.

In her many attempts to have children with that damn Adam, various creatures were born.

The first litters were grotesque. The newborns didn't understand where their legs should go, or that they were for getting around.

Eve was developing the idea of what her offspring ought to be and what she ought to be, too. First, she succeeded in becoming who she is, and then she conceived us, in her image and likeness.

Because the fact that they had hooves when they left Eden is just as true as some other things that she left out so we wouldn't doubt her. She lied because she was wary and modest, which is not her natural way, but she has strong social instincts and knows what to say and what not to say to hold our interest. The truth is that she and Adam were both farcical beings before achieving the beauty they think they embody. They left Eden half formed, the apple only set them on the path of desire, they were still misshapen when they set their hooves upon the Earth. In a way, they are their own children, they created themselves. Before giving themselves life, they dragged their hands on the ground when they walked.

Before us, there were also wonderful generations.

THEN ADAM SAID:
The first woman appeared long after men did. They made her out of the abundant water and earth. With what was left over from molding her body, they made a vessel and a lid.

When they had finished forming her figure, they showered her with gifts: beauty, musical skill, eloquence, ingenuity, powerful imagination. Then, in the vessel they made at the same time—from the remnants of her clay—they put all the evils of the world and sealed it with the clay lid.

The first woman knew that this vessel, her companion, should remain shut. But curiosity got the best of her, and one day she opened it: that's where the evil that condemns us to misery came from.

It was Eve's fault.

MORE FROM ADAM:
"When he prepared to make Eve, the one whom we should not name said, 'I won't make her from Adam's head because she would arise, arrogant; I won't make her from Adam's eye because she'll look at everything, inattentive; I won't make her from his neck

because she'd be impudent; I won't make her from his mouth because she would talk too much; I won't make her from his heart because she'd be jealous; I won't make her from his hand because she'd end up being meddlesome; and I certainly won't make her from his foot because she'd be a wanderer; I chose to make her from a rib so she would turn out to be chaste.' Despite these precautions, the woman turned out to have all these defects—gossipy, loudmouthed, insolent, arrogant, peripatetic, and, on top of all that, slutty."

MORE:
(The daughters of Eve who say "I was my own other half" are disgusting; I was a complete being. Unlike Adam and my brothers, with their inside-out intestine, always worrying about finding hides to cover it up. Sticking it everywhere, in goats, magnolia flowers, women (whether they were fully grown or not), the fish Eve was going to stew, the hogs, the cormorants (if they let them), anywhere at all (and in their desperation, even the hedgehog, nibbling on grass); alas, always trying to clothe their naked things. Not me: I always had it covered, my little tongue of pleasure ever safe between the lips between my legs, as wise as the tongue in my mouth.")

ANOTHER PAPER WITH A NOTE, POSSIBLY EVE'S:
Life is coming to an end. In his fury, Cain destroyed cruel cities that embodied Abel's spirit as opposed to that of the vegetables and fruits he had planted and grown.

Red blood ran through the gutters of the city. Its inhabitants hungered for death. And so, war was born of Abel's rage, Cain's plunder, Abel's guile, Adam's lies. It had nothing to do with me.

And in order that this not be forgotten, I'll record it here: "The serpent is the force of good who looks after the water beneath the earth."

And something else I think I've never said before: "Hair that has been let down is wrath."

CAIN'S DREAM:
Adam, who was my father, accidentally decapitated one of his children and mistakenly put an elephant's head in its place.

ANOTHER PAPER, TITLED "PARENTHESIS" (BECAUSE THAT'S WHAT IT IS):
(I have never tired of looking at the light of the Moon shining in silver and shadow, always a nuanced reflection of light. By contrast, the harshness of the Sun paralyzes me (especially when, high above, it leaves us without a hint of shade, bereft of companions, its eternal and inquisitive eye eliminating all doubt).

Abel and Adam spoke ill of the Moon, unaware that their worship of the Sun was that of a cruel being.)

(How did common sense abandon the Earth for other lands? Is that true, or is the wording imprecise? Was any prudence left behind? Beneath the waters of the seas, rocked gently by the Earth's crust, the most bizarre things were unleashed, creatures assumed unheard-of shapes, their size exceeding all precedent. When the Sun was closest to her, Earth, a hypocrite, displayed bodies and behavior that were, if not logical, less grotesque.)

(Abel should have been the one that died. So say I, Eve. I, who, through maternal bonds, should feel the same deep and abiding attachment to each of my offspring. But even if a mother could feel that way, it would be impossible in the case of Cain and Abel. Because whoever gives birth to Cain and then Abel is forced to choose a side. For Cain or against Cain. Which is less painful? It's less decent to take the part of Abel, the butcher. I didn't know that when I chose Cain, I chose pain; everything indicated it would be to the contrary.

There's a lesson here: for their mothers every child is forever an open wound.)

(I should add: with his absurd stories Adam planted the seed, ignited the flame that made raping women a right, a necessity, a pleasure, and even a joy, and justified the murder of more than one—beautiful but nameless—only on account of their gender.

Because of his widely accepted tales we females became like sand, targets of the violence that was the very foundation of their beings. Men.

I never should have held my tongue when I had things to say. Never.)

ANOTHER OF ADAM'S:
When they saw me, newly created, great in my perfect solitude, the animals in the sea, the ones that slither, walk, run, and fly or glide through the strata of the heavens, the giants and even the angels all believed I was their master and prepared to greet me with a "Holy, Holy, Holy is the Lord of Pilgrims," clearing their throats, when He saw the error that would cause the damnation of all living things and put me to sleep, and then the angels knew that I was nothing but a human being.

ANOTHER OF ADAM'S:
When I gave in to temptation, when Eve induced me to sin, He said to me, "Adam, Adam, you have abandoned me! I shall abandon you, too! We'll see what you can manage all on your own!"[5]

---

5. Imre Madách, *The Tragedy of Man*, trans. George Szirtes (Budapest: Corvina, 1988).

ANOTHER PAPER OF EVE'S (WHICH APPEARS TO GO
WITH A PAGE FROM BOOK SIX):

When I brought angels into the world, I took them where Abel,
the first of the dead, was resting. I left them there and returned
home.

When I leaned over the well in the patio some days later, I
heard them horsing around with him. I knew they were happy
with Abel. At last, they had a male among their ranks.

I also knew that Abel didn't realize he was dead, and that that
had been the case for a long time.

BOOK SEVEN

67

Cain's Exile

Adam got rid of Cain, conveying the "curse" from his god. Cain hurried away into exile. He took a pinch of the starter dough, a variety of seeds (fresh, toasted, hulled, and whole), nuts, roots. He took his jug, full of water, two of the dogs from the house, a blanket, the beautiful wheel he had just made, a donkey. He put a board for making a table on the donkey's back, and two chairs.

He took the most precious thing with him—words—although I kept them, too, in duplicate. With those words, he took my memory, too. Unfortunately, he also took some of Adam's words, because he accidentally took the talking splinter I had pulled from the ruined dough, which had gotten mixed in with the seeds.

Adah went with him, which was my greatest loss.

68

Abel's Body

Cain and Adah's departure was such a blow that my clitoris dried up. I heard it rustle at night, trying to get comfortable, like a stiff thing that lacked moisture. As though that damn talking splinter had stuck there, and once imbedded, fallen silent.

I don't attribute this change to Abel's corpse, or the fact that I didn't attend to it. I knew that it would have the same fate as any other dead body. I watched it, beginning on the second day, when the flies and other insects approached to feed on it. That I could not allow. Abel might be Abel, he might be the child I gave to Adam, but no matter what he was, he was the fruit of my loins, he had learned to speak words and was the brother of my other children, he had eaten at my table.

Before going on about Abel's body I should add that war had been declared between Adam and Eve:

We've been sitting here for centuries, meditating ferociously
how to deal the one last blow that will finally
annihilate the other one forever.[6]

I thought about burying it to avoid witnessing its decay right before my eyes. But the idea upset me, I didn't want to feel "the

---

6. Rosario Castellanos, "*Ajedrez*" ("Chess"), in *A Rosario Castellanos Reader*, (Austin: University of Texas Press, 2010).

bitter delight of your slumber, below, upon your bed of earth."[7] I set about creating a shelter for my Abel's body. I said to him: "This clay, touched by my hand, these flames, in which I will fire it, and the silent heat of this stone oven will be your companions underground.

"My son: the worms shall not eat your body, it will not crumble like sand, nor shall it nourish vultures and crows. I, who brought you into this world, will keep you safe in the night of a cave. I shall make a clay vessel for your body. I shall carry you to your final home."

I got to work. I cleaned Abel's body. In our horror at what had happened we had avoided touching it and it had become stiff, bent in the position it had been in when Cain brought it to me on his back. I carefully removed his intestines with a bone knife and put him in the sun to preserve him while I shaped and fired a vessel to put him in. I handled a knife well: when all was said and done, I was the butcher's mother, and I learned his trade with a heavy heart.

I fit Abel's body into this bespoke vessel and covered it with a lid big enough to be decorated with the silhouettes of my two male children, one with a donkey's jawbone in his hand. I tied the vessel holding Abel to my back and began to walk. I resolved to make it to the first snowy peak of that intricate, original mountain range, whence we had come.

My plan was to carry him where his body wouldn't decay and find him a big cavern, but if I couldn't find one then at least a cave or a niche to shelter him from the goats and bears and birds of prey because his body had the odor of dead meat despite my disemboweling it and laying it in the sun to desiccate.

---

7. "*Siento el amargo goce de que duermas abajo / en tu lecho de tierra.*" Fragment from Gabriela Mistral, "Poema del hijo.".

My two youngest daughters came with me, carrying sheep skins (some of the ones Abel had torn from his livestock, drying them and stockpiling them) to cover us when the cold began to lash us, as well as provisions, though not much remained after Cain's departure, but at least we had something.

We walked and talked but when we reached the first slope we climbed in silence. A voracious, implacable wind accompanied us. The younger of my two daughters made booties out of the sheep skins to protect our naked feet. We wore hides, taking care to leave the vessel with Abel's body exposed so the cold would preserve him.

No sooner were the slopes covered in snow than we were in luck: we found a medium-sized cave whose opening was like a twisted mouth, sheltering it from the wind. We entered and built a fire.

On the dark, black walls I depicted Adah's night of terror, Abel's erect penis, and Adam's timid but excited one behind his two children.

My daughters sang. We didn't dance. We waited for dawn to arrive to embark upon our return journey, and then we set off. We hadn't gone far before a storm began to rage. We returned to the cave, sharing it with the cadaver. We sang. We did not dance. I did not draw anything, sensing that perhaps that was what had summoned the storm.

As soon as the tempest allowed, we left. The path was slippery, and the wind was treacherous because it blew when we least expected it. Our descent was painfully slow. We no longer had anything left to eat. We did as Abel would have when we saw the cubs of feral creatures, which we roasted at dusk on our nightly fire.

I retold the complete truth to my daughters. I imagined that, in our absence, foulmouthed Adam had continued embellishing his lie.

My clitoris seemed to have come back to life.

69

Barren Earth

A greater grief awaited us. Earth—as they explained when we returned—was angered by Cain's absence. Recalcitrant, it bore blighted fruit—stoneless, naked, empty (fragile, thin membranes in the place of skin, flesh desiccated or absent from lack of protection). This is all true, but it could have been remedied.

There were no more budding flowers; as soon as they blossomed their leaves disappeared, their stalks shriveled, hardened, and dried out, their roots dissolving in the dry earth. This is all true, but it could have been remedied.

The white darkness of the spores was tinged with gray; the branch of the river that protected us dried up; the earth was sterile; it did not rain; the brook disappeared; the bees left for a better home; the pastures bore no corn or wheat; the lean trees let fall their bark in sticky drops the insects fled from; the river that had run nearby became a stagnant quagmire and then a dry bed: this is all true, but it could have been remedied.

Our hunger was not like the giants', which isn't born of the need for nourishment—because they wanted to eat but they did not, they thirsted to drink, but did not.

We were condemned to dig for root vegetables to sate our hunger. But when we found them, they, too, had been touched by misfortune—they were like our own flesh, there was nothing there to eat, as though our famished spirits had devoured them before we dug them up.

This all could have been remedied. Hunger and thirst made themselves at home in our abode; Adam didn't lift a finger. He had let the crops, the fruits of so much effort, die. Earth wouldn't do her part if we didn't do ours. In our absence, Adam had spent all his time refining his version of events.

My spirit was crestfallen, agitated, shaken up—I was like a single drop of my former self—shapeless, the energy sapped from my bones. Or rather, I was like a dried-up drop; the skies of my joy failed to provide a single droplet, like those on Earth.

There was nothing in the house but hunger and thirst—and my profound sadness, which left no room for fertility or pleasure or even yearning for them.

We had no sooner arrived than hunger forced us to move on, to leave our home, abandoning the withered crops. We needed seeds to be able to feed ourselves. We had become like the Cainites forced into exile, but without hardworking Cain or any supplies. The only thing we didn't lack was the talking splinter of bone, because Adam was the splinter—though he was a living being he, too, overflowed with resentment. He had let his hair grow wild. He insisted that we women cover ours, too, but we ignored him.

We knew from before that we ought not to go near the river or follow its course for fear of being slaughtered by the beasts that lived there. Now that there were more of us the fire wouldn't suffice to keep our scent from predators. The animals that belonged to Abel's followers, a variety of livestock, came with us; though they walked on their own legs, and some carried the weight of our belongings on their backs, they were just more mouths to feed. Discord reigned among them—the ostrich and her offspring fought for food; they didn't realize we were all vagabonds united by a common cause.

Some of the animals devoured one another.

Seth was born of my loins, my son by Adam, from a night

of recriminations that culminated in my humiliation and defeat. Seth was just another desperate mouth to feed. I called Seth the Fearful One because he was wary, he knew how to fear, and he was unashamed to show it.

70

Beer

Fortunately, we had beer and other spirits. Only when we drank did we feel human again, able to forget our circumstances; alcohol allowed us to wax lyrical, imagining, seeing the beauty of Earth.

Alcohol also made our troupe lazier and more irritable, and, as I've said, forgetful. I have no idea who was mating with whom. I had more children—how quickly they grew in our hopeless wandering, full of evil, captive to vice; and with the same ferocity as that ostrich I saw fighting with its offspring, they fought among themselves over everything.

It still had not rained a drop and everything green had turned yellow, as if it were burnt. The trees fell. The jealous streams had strangled all their inhabitants. The air burned and hardly moved.

Since we were so many and so hungry as we moved from place to place, dragging our few possessions along with our desperate souls, and had no livestock left, I went out hunting to feed us all, because I felt a responsibility to provide. I killed with spears. I killed with stones.

We were in such a state of amnesia that at first we ate raw meat. The wretched flesh of vipers restored our strength. We gnawed on bones. I dedicated myself to hunting. I was the lioness. Adam looked after my cubs. Adam became more talkative, more violent. He insisted upon his version of events. He convinced the troops born during our wanderings. I didn't speak much; I gave birth, hunted, roasted my prey on the fire; we ate without plates, no table, no bread; I had become the living picture of hopelessness.

Alcohol put me into a deep sleep with vivid dreams. I'll share one here, which I dreamed when I was drunk and half covered in blood after fighting the cub of an enormous beast which I defeated with my bare hands after wounding it with the bone tip of my spear, and which I dismembered without the aid of any knife:

71

The Dream of the Homunculi

Sun scalded skin. I couldn't find a way to refill the water jugs. Thirst tormented me. I drank foamy liquid, a fermented drink, setting the fruit rinds aside.

I fell into a heavy, restless sleep. The men returned before my daughters did. Seeing me lying there, unmoving (but snoring loudly in my agitation), they expelled as much semen as possible, beneath the pitiless Sun's bright light. That's how I saw them, rubbing themselves and ejaculating, when I jerked awake.

I did not awaken alone: at the same time homunculi awoke from the semen, dozens of tiny men, each carrying a bow: a giant swollen penis. So big they would have fallen over face-first if it weren't for the quivers full of arrows on their backs. Their skinny legs were always spread, as if the quivers alone weren't heavy enough to keep them upright.

When they took aim they gave little leaps, agile as sparks, as though the floor were ejecting them instead of supporting them. They appeared to have no skin, but they were as smooth as if they had been carved out of wood, their flesh hard, nearly rigid.

One homunculus took the string from his bow. One end of the string was so stiff it had a point, an awl. He approached me, brandishing it, he looked ridiculous with that swollen blade wobbling ahead of him, completely out of proportion—as long as a third leg but larger than his four extremities combined. Some other homunculi grabbed me by the ankles. I was surprised by their strength. Whatever they were made of—this species of hard-wood—was like a weapon. Some other homunculi climbed onto my body, tying down my arms, torso, face.

The homunculus who held the awl-thread stepped onto my face. He entered my mouth. He pierced my tongue. I wanted to say *Ow!* but the pain was intense, and it would have made no difference; he anchored the thread there, left my mouth, and with that awl-point of the thread he proceeded to sew my lips together. He double stitched and knotted the thread firmly to seal my mouth shut.

He left me mute, voiceless.

I heard the songs of my daughters approaching our home. I watched the homunculi release the strings of their bows simultaneously, weaving them into a net *in an instant*. When they pulled at the net's edges it expanded. Then the homunculi disappeared from sight; only the net remained, stretched lengthwise across the entrance to the house.

My daughters, happy and carefree, continued singing; our mare, Cloud (her dark mane, her spotted coat, her white tail bouncing), pulled a cart full of flowers, fruits, jugs of fresh water. Behind them, at a distance, I spotted the second group, the ones who were returning from visiting the city in their covered wagon pulled by two mules, full of goods from the market: fabrics, thread (quite different from that of the homunculi), perfumed oils, trinkets, things from the city.

The first group approached the net. Happy at the sight of our home, they began to dance to their song, clapping. Perceiving danger, the mare moved backward and began to circle, neighing. They ignored her, one of the girls took her crop and her whip, calmed her down and untethered her from the cart, holding her by the bit and the harness. Ever loyal, the steed bent its legs and knelt. I understood her reaction: she saw the danger but, since we had enslaved her, the rebelliousness inside her had been suppressed.

I thought, *You and I, faithful Cloud, my girl—the doorway!* reciting in my head, *we won't get caught in the doorway, we won't get caught in the doorway, we won't get caught in the doorway,* which belied the situation I was in—all tied up.

My daughters got caught in the net like insects in a spiderweb.

It wasn't a dream, I was awake.

Then a homunculus chose one of the girls. He didn't completely free her from the web, just enough so that he could have her, and since she was unable to move, he made her with child right then and there. In Abel's world that's how the children were: two parts male and only one (immobile) part female.

They cut off our voices, every last one.

The same night that I dreamed about the homunculi Adam had this dream:

Eve, more beautiful than ever, young and smiling, came over to where he lay sleeping, caressed him, and began to eat him, starting with his fingers and hands, next his forearms and arms, going on and on, advancing through her meal while she birthed a child with her splendid body, no sweat, no pain.

END OF BOOK SEVEN

Mixed loose pages

ONE OF ADAM'S:
It wasn't my idea to send my firstborn, Cain, into exile. I was ordered to. "The blood of your kin cries out from the earth," He told me—so loudly that everyone must have heard it.

A PAGE:
Following Cain's example—not Abel's—Seth (the Fearful One) warily departed our ranks and founded a city. Some say it was Mecca.

ANOTHER PAGE:
Since I didn't have my voice, I set to work making a new one. Mute, I made thread and wove it to make a braid; by weaving the braid crosswise I made fabric; the fabric had surface, texture. I soon learned how to live on the fabric, as a figure on a piece of cloth. The threads wound around me, they *were* me, in my speechlessness I had gone to live there in softness and color, I had blossoms, stalks, sand, and sometimes even the heat of a fire.

ANOTHER:
I'll weave Eve's story. I have decided to be her voice. She wasn't allowed to weave it herself. They cut off her voice violently. What she was saying and the thread of her story were broken.

Eve's thread was made from different fibers. Hers is a costly silence. I want to fix it.

She was wild in her desperation, her desperation not to be silenced.

Alas, silence. A simple word. A noose. A word that lies because it's said to be essential for survival when the opposite is true. "Shut up and you'll live"; what a twisted, evil thing to say.

And in her case, what purpose did it serve?

ANOTHER FROM ONE OF EVE'S DAUGHTERS (WHO, IN TRUTH, SEEMS A BIT CRAZY):
Some time ago Eve founded a village of women. It was the place where we females went to give birth. It had steam baths and burial grounds for the unlucky; twelve-month-old boys were sacrificed so their bodies could serve as lids for the tombs, facedown toward the center of the Earth. Some boys under the age of two were buried farther underground, with green stones in their mouths to keep their souls from escaping, making their sacrifice pointless. Sacrifice, a magical practice.

The green stones in the mouths of those sacrificed children were useless, because a soul can't escape from a mouth that hasn't pronounced a word, and they were too young to say a whole one.

A PAGE OF EVE'S:
At sea, the one singing aboard a ship is my daughter, with her three-stringed instrument.

She, too, feared Abel.

BOOK EIGHT

72

It Rained

It rained. By then I had completely lost all sense of time and space. When the rain began, I didn't know whether we had wandered astray or whether we had never moved at all. We were in an unrecognizable place.

Numerous animal skulls sat atop the skeletons of dry, bald trees, exposed to the sun. Not a single live animal from our herds remained, not even a dog or a cat. The fields showed no sign of ever being ploughed. There was no grass either; the earth was barren, like lumpy, pale sand. Our sense of abandonment was immense. The gentle rain urged us to recover and renew our joy and vitality.

But not everyone. The majority of us seemed inclined to lead miserable lives.

We women got to work. We cleared the land of stones, hid the carcasses, rescued some dormant seeds—some of which even looked like they were sprouting, thanks to the rain.

The rain continued.

73

Adam's Illness and Death

Adam fell ill. He prayed to his "He, the Divine"—foundering, drowning in the damp, solid earth, as if the gift of rain was a showering death upon him. I wondered, *How to ask Thunder for something?* as I listened to him plead feverishly to be healed, whenever he stopped repeating, "Eve, stop eating me." He was in such a state that I invoked the angels.

The Archangel Michael appeared, clothed like us, no brilliance, no fire. He spoke to Adam, telling him his prayers were useless, that he was sick, that he was going to die because we were mortal, that no one would escape that fate, until the Son of Man was born, and that he should prepare for death.

Later Adam claimed that the Archangel said something different: that we would all die because of me, because I had tasted the apple, that in one bite I had made us all mortal beings. He also said that Seth and I had accompanied him to the gates of Heaven (?), passing through Eden (?), and that we should anoint his body so that he would be admitted when his time came. I took this last thing into consideration; everything else was just part of his great lie.

That was the last time I saw the Archangel Michael.

When Adam died, his fantasy—his lie—gained strength a hundredfold. Once dead he was ever present. The walls of the living no longer contained his breath; rather, they enhanced it, like a magnifying glass. His malign tale floated around and stuck there, promoting a climate of rancor and violence. The iniquity of our progeny was great; and the place where we women were confined was an abomination. My dream of the homunculi was nothing compared to my actual life. We had water and food, shelter and companionship, but the level of hostility made it hard for me to breathe.

Each time a newborn was placed in its crib, a chalk circle surrounding the words *Adam and Eve. Lilith begone!* was drawn on it. I abandoned all hope of the truth prevailing. I thought another fantasy might convince them. Since everything female was viewed as evil, I changed my name to Hebe and drew a woman riding a lion on the entrance to my tent; I carved it in stone, too. That story *did* leave my lips; it wasn't my own story, but it captured my essence.

On one of my outings, they shattered my sculpture of Hebe and spread mud all over the drawing on my tent. When I returned, they all shouted, "You'll never worship an idol again!" And one yelled, "Women begone! Death to worthless women!"

We changed our manner of dress, choosing long, loose skirts. We painted our lips red. We covered our chests with fabric that made our breasts look larger. We wore colorful shoes. Our clitorises laughed beneath our garments. Children seemed to sprout more rapidly inside us and when they were born, we helped each other raise them, providing each other with companionship, and our red mouths laughed, too. We talked and talked. We danced. Music filled our days.

The men went out hunting. We felt no desire whatsoever to join them. While they hunted, we formed a community that prolonged our children's childhood; it was taking them longer and longer to grow up, and they became more and more like Eve when she was awakening in Eden. Today I think: Cain's generation experienced no infancy. Neither Abel nor Adah nor their two sisters. Their children took two years to mature. Enoch's children took three. At this point, they were taking nine, they needed all that time to develop.

Looking after the children was time-consuming. And it gave us deep pleasure.

The men stayed away from our nurturing circle of joy. They returned from hunting in a frame of mind that made them even more distant. Their hunts had become savage. What was the point of shooting a heron full of arrows and celebrating its death by ululating around its cadaver? Or the point of playing with the remains of everything they killed? That's just one example. Or of wearing their feathers, sticking them on with blood, or donning their flayed skins, which looked like the ones wrought by brutal Thunder? Those are just a few of the things they did. In our camp there was more violence, too, until being male became equated with causing pain.

(Men and women—alas!—so devious. The Cancer of the World.)

In light of this, I did something I had done long ago, when I relinquished my way of making children to make Adam feel better: I took a step back and had some compassion for them—poor men, left out of the fun and games!

It had become customary that when night fell the men sat apart from the women, drawing up rules governing the ownership of land and us women, fighting about their "rights" over this or that (woman or piece of land). They began to enforce them with punitive measures, making laws in which our hands were tied, so to speak.

They controlled the barter of foodstuffs, forbidding women to exchange food with one another; even tiny seeds had to pass through a man's hands before they could enter our cooking pots. The rumor spread that if a woman who was menstruating went near the fields, the crops and the fruits would dry up, and this confabulation stuck fast to us like tar floating in salt water, so that we could no longer farm, either. They made up another whopper that if a woman went out alone, she would become evil, removing her legs at night and sucking the blood of babies; that one stuck, too, because they had spread their fear throughout the community. The dream that Adam had when I had mine about the homunculi had lodged in each man's chest, and when they exhaled their fear, it spread like contagion. They feared us because we could give life, because we looked after the cooking and the cadavers; they feared our red lips and our beauty, they feared their attraction to us and the boundless pleasure we experienced.

Our hair was kept hidden according to the laws of the community, using cadavers' hair (or horsehair), which was braided to look like ours. Our mouths stopped being red. Our skirts turned gray and black, and we lost the ability to dance. Our shoes lost their color. We wore corsets. Some men forced "their" women to wear chastity belts. We lost half of our names. We had no right to own property. Children were named after their fathers even though we were still responsible for looking after them. They used sharp stones to excise the clitoris of more than one little girl to make her "pure" "for her whole life"—though not by tying them down (as in my dream of the homunculi), but by restraining them. They took our children from us during the day because they thought we couldn't educate them and designated one of their own as "the teacher," who told them what was good and what was bad, what to do and what not to do. They made up all sorts of rules about good manners and bad manners. They imposed them on all our households. And then the next blow came: the girls—with or without clitorises—weren't allowed to attend school. They stayed home, shut in with their mothers, subjected to arcane rules. And if they went out in the streets, it was never without a chaperone, and the girls and their mothers had to veil their bodies and faces. For chaperones, they castrated the men who didn't enjoy their violent games, the ones deemed "weakest."

Some of the men who played these violent games kept a chosen group of women. Their bodies were manipulated to look like caricatures: monstrously large breasts, waistlines smaller than any corset could create, protruding bottoms. Some could barely stand, their breasts were so large; others suffered from terrible back pain. They were prohibited from touching their clitorises; they were filled with unguents so they could be penetrated without feeling any pleasure; they were forced to dance naked. The men made them parade around at their gatherings and inside their tents, where we were forbidden to enter.

And from time to time, they killed a woman, using the same brutal methods of butchery that had become the norm for the animals. They killed women because their skirts were too stiff, or because they went out alone, dragging them out of their homes. None of us were safe, not even those of us without a clitoris—who were now in the majority—breasts or no breasts, mothers or childless, young or old. And they called this pleasure. It supplanted true pleasure. The wonder and love of life was supplanted by their thirst for violence and hunger for blood, their resentment, their hate.

Cooking and dining together, which had always been a convivial source of joy, became two very different experiences: the dinner table became an extension of school, governed by rules—no one spoke except the fathers. As for the fireplace and the cooking pots, they were all we had left. Cooking was no longer one of our great joys—something we had shared with the Earth; it had become associated exclusively with hunting. The men, who governed everything outside our tents, had practically abandoned the fields apart from cultivating the grain for our bread, which they decreed had to be unleavened. All we ate was cadavers.

Adam's version of events had won. It didn't happen immediately; it gathered power in the way of "this is our tradition."

The ones who were a real nightmare were my grandchildren and great-grandchildren, whom I had known from birth and whom I had cared for when they were young, as each successive generation took longer to grow up. The ones who had been my happiness. The ones who had once known the secrets of the clitoris, the language of that wise and clever little tongue. They became deaf to the language of pleasure.

These, our young ones, tied our hands; I won't go on because I have no desire to return there, even in memory. Tied by our hands—but not our feet.

74

Eve's Flight from Her Flock

I could no longer stand living with such a flock. One night I left home in the middle of the night.

I didn't tell any of my daughters or granddaughters about my departure; I had lost faith in the ones I had once trusted. How could I have trusted them, hidden as they were beneath shawls, stiff and heavy dark dresses, and woolen socks, their faces hardened by resentment?

The dogs didn't bark because they knew me, and I threw them scraps; I whistled and called them by name. Two even followed me, and I let them; I'd need them later. I brought along a pair of each of the animals Seth, the Fearful One, had domesticated.

As I set out on my journey that night, I captured more animals with my lasso. My dogs helped, as well as the animals I had just captured. I chose the best ones, a male and female of each species.

The river nearby was flowing once more. On its banks I built a boat—I didn't know how to build one, but I did know how to build a house, and it was just a case of putting the roof on the bottom, floating instead of sheltering, that did the trick!—and, without thinking twice, I got into my boat with my animals—the domesticated ones and the ones I had captured that very night on my journey to the riverbank, and the ones I continued to capture, night after night, roping the eagles and other creatures as they slept.

It continued to rain.

In my boat I'd be able to leave behind the vicious race with whom I had nothing in common.

I hoped to reunite with my sweet Cain in his city.

75

Cain's City

I knew thanks to a messenger who had arrived around the time the rains began: while we wasted away during the famine, reduced to almost nothing, Cain had a child and founded a city he named after this son, Enoch—who, when he had grown, was known as the wisest and most just man that ever lived. It was said that Cain was cursed, that he could never die. Could it be true? According to the Archangel Michael that was impossible, but I had faith he was still alive and that he would recognize me and that I would be able to make a new home where he was, in his city, governed according to his custom and the wisdom of his son Enoch.

From the moment I boarded my boat the rain didn't cease. It was good; the river rose, and its current grew stronger. And since I didn't know how to steer a boat the river carried me along. Once again, Earth had generously looked after me, this time with one of her many thousands of waterways.

It was fresh water. Full of schools of fish yearning to be eaten by me, surrounding me so that I didn't even need to use a net or hook to bring them aboard and set them out to dry; I scooped them up in a bucket and laid them out on deck, their tails slapping, eager for the peace of my cooking pot.

The river widened. The schools of fish swam deeper and were harder to reach. On the banks I saw the enormous beasts Adam and I had fled from so long ago. Beasts that were formidable even at a distance: elephants, rhinoceroses, leopards, lions, huge birds of prey with giant beaks filled with rows of sharp teeth. They could no longer attack me, even though my boat was full of delicious things for them to eat. Enormous crocodiles tried to capsize my boat, whipping their tails, but the river came to my defense, forming thick braids with its turbulent and unpredictable currents.

And before we began to weaken or run out of provisions, and without much of an effort, we docked at the port of the city of Enoch, in the Land of Nod.

END OF BOOK EIGHT

Loose papers (containing The Book of Cain, as well as others)

FROM ADAM:
And Adam said:

". . . the children of God, the angels, were sent to Earth to teach humans what was right and what was true. They taught Enoch, Cain's son, the secrets of Heaven and Earth. They had been made lustful by the perfidious daughters of man, lazy women from the land of Eve and from the Land of Nod, expert in the art of painting their faces, perfuming, and adorning themselves to seduce and corrupt with their wiles.

"Using their angelic beauty, they had their way with virgins, matrons, other men, and even animals because they could not contain their lust.

"Even before the angels fell into turpitude there weren't many virgins left, because the women had given in to their carnal desires. The angels were so handsome, and the women were so dissolute (and beautiful) that in no time there was only one virgin left: Ishtahar.

"Ishtahar was not just another sweetie. The angels found her irresistible because her purity made her the most beautiful of all. One after another, they tried everything they could to corrupt her. But she was as clever as a man, or one of Abel's descendants; she didn't say *yes* or *no* but she made a demand: 'I'd happily be thine but first, lend me your wings!'

"One foolish angel was so eager to have her that he gave her his wings. The moment she got them, Ishtahar put them on and flew away, crossing the Heavens to touch the white flesh of Dawn (so like her own) and rising even higher, up to God's throne. There she settled in Dawn's lap, like a dove in its nest. The Creator, whose name you are not worthy to speak, knew she was a woman, and even though she was a virgin, he took a swipe at her to get rid of her.

"Tossed into the vast emptiness, Ishtahar grabbed on to the first thing she could and became the constellation of Virgo."

Thus shall it be written.

EVE'S PAPERS:
Our surroundings were full of animals four times our height, an abundance of colorful feathers, intricately patterned skins, long necks, and immense, sturdy hooves. They were docile and clever—or wily and tricky; they lived off of us.

Cain wouldn't have let them get that big. Abel would have bred them to become stronger and more cunning and brought them to our table, boasting about the hunt, though it took place in his corral.

Above water: jaws. Below water: more jaws. Teeth all over the earth, prideful, rapacious teeth, all lined up to devour our flesh; there was nothing else in sight worth eating. The ones whose hides were shiny and smooth were the most deceptive of all.

Alas. Those long necks on massive bodies, elegant and handsome. Their long legs were deceptive, too.

The Book of Cain

I was born to till the soil. I was exiled from my homeland because of brotherly ties, condemned for killing one who decided we were rivals. Those who say I "brought forth greed, envy, hate, and crime"[8] are wrong. How foolish and absurd.

---

8. Juana de Ibarbourou, "*Caín*" ("Cain"), in *Estampas de la Biblia* (Buenos

I loved seeds, flowers, and the vegetables I grew, which nourished us with beauty, sweet scents, and delicious flavors. I devised a schedule for sowing and reaping. We grew delicious fruit, lovely flowers. The seeds became larger, tree branches learned to be grafted, creating wonders. Our orchard was a paradise. Eve's first child, the horse, procreated, making more animals who helped us work the land.

With Eve I learned to shape clay and manage fire, so we could make vessels for the seeds and the dishes she prepared.

From dusk to dawn we attended to our duties conscientiously, despite the blinding sunlight; we followed the vagaries of the crazy Moon, and together we watched the stars to try to understand what on earth they were saying.

Sometimes when we were up late on lookout Eve told us about how we had come to be here, describing all the different things that came to pass, because nothing in memory remains ungrafted, and her stories—like the things we grew—made us tremble with delight. Everyone knows that those who are sensitive are fragile, and those who are insensitive are impervious.

We built a house. We drew, we learned how to make music with reeds; stones provided us protection.

I was even more mild-natured than Eve because she attended to all my needs and wants. I was hers, her Cain, her firstborn son, her collaborator.

Abel was different. He despised working nonstop, and he preferred amusing himself to getting things done. He went out with the animals to graze, to watch them and gaze

Aires: Ediciones de la Sociedad Amigos del Libro Rioplatense, 1934).

at the sky. His head was empty. And empty heads develop a taste for blood. He killed one animal after another. To taunt us he threw them on our fire, giving us the dead to eat. He killed more and more. Soon he saw the animals only as his prey.

We preferred embers; Abel, open flames.

Abel was Adam's son. He planted him in Eve's hindquarters when she was sleeping. I was born of Eve's pleasure, Abel of Adam's rage. Adam enjoyed everything that was born of the unpleasantness he and Abel shared. Eve's son, I shared her vitality and tenacity; Adah, who was both Eve's and mine, had those qualities twice over.

Abel didn't like to sleep indoors. He had no interest in hearing the stories we told at night. He was bored by clay; he drank from other things: bladders, entrails, horns, and even skins, where he stored the fresh water he came across on his ramblings.

We used the things he drank from and left behind— forgetting even to burn them—to make music. The bladders made a harmonious sound. The lungs made a deeper, mournful sound. He used the hides of animals he skinned without slitting them from top to bottom. Their viscera made strings (there will never be more perfect ones than these, though others would throw them away). We held concerts with these castoffs.

There was a lot between Abel and me, we were brothers. As newborns we suckled from the same breast; as little boys we played while Eve worked and Adam nursed his anger, a whole forest of angers, in which I did not lose myself. I chose Eve, just as she chose me.

Adah chose us both, as brothers, Abel and me. And we both wanted her. But Adah wanted me.

I would never have chosen to leave my vegetable garden, the fruit trees, the variety of fields I planted surrounding our house. I would never have chosen to go with Adam that morning to offer what he called a sacrifice. I agreed because I never imagined that we, his sons, would be sacrificed to his rage. And I would certainly never have wanted to stain my hands with blood in an outburst of fury with Abel.

And even less than that for Abel to force himself upon Adah, my sister, my daughter, my wife. To wound her in revenge for something that did not call for vengeance.

Thus was I thrown into this life I didn't seek. First, wandering and exile. In my own way I repeated Adam's fall, but not Eve's adventure. Later, after founding the first city (another thing I did not set out to do), I dreamed that it was peopled only with honest men, a refuge from the giants and the Nephilim, their evil progeny with my sisters, who lived for inflicting pain and death, as if they were the flesh of Abel's flesh.

The Nephilim who never eat and always hunger. Who wound and damage.

But they weren't the only wicked ones. The sons of men and women far surpassed Abel.

The flesh of Abel's flesh: he was a glutton for the living, the killer, the drinker of blood. In his corral he lays a boar on its back and cuts its throat with his stone knife; a fountain of dark blood springs from the wound, Abel leans over the open vein and drinks. He removes his mouth and covers the wound with the bladder of another swine, filling it with blood.

We used the same bladders to make music, without blood.

I, Abel, say: My parents were covered up by Yahweh, to hide the nakedness of original sin. And that is why they were also covered in the blood of freshly flayed beasts, to expiate them. And that is why Man must continue to dress as such: the purity of the animals he eats and wears reminds him daily of Eve's sin, seducing us just as the serpent seduced her. Eve—the greatest of all serpents, and womankind, too. The reason why childbirth causes pain.

Someone will write: Adam means "red" because he was made from earth that color. Eve means "mother of all peoples." Cain, "possession." Abel, "sorrow."

Adam gave me a lot of different seeds and a piece of the mother dough so that when harvest time came, I could continue eating bread.

He didn't give me any of the mother alcohol, but he did give me some of the mother vinegar.

I brought two blankets with me to protect us from the cold at night.

Weevils ate the seeds before I could put them to rest underground.

Flying ants attacked the mother dough; it was so full of their dead bodies that it became useless.

The blankets Eve made from fibers and flowers were eaten by moths.

All I had left was the vinegar.

As the poet said:

> Ay, the survivor,
> he who rots in broad daylight, grave
> wide open,
> suitor of stenches and worms
>
> . . .
>
> Condemned to life![9]

This wicked race identified with Adam's convictions. They excelled Abel in their cruelty. They devised a way to slaughter many animals at once—to feed the growing population, they'd say—and there are no words for how they butchered them, making use of every part of their bodies, stuffing the dead animals into their own intestines to preserve them. Their wickedness redoubled when they thought this made the food more delectable.

Death: the recreation of the Abelites. In all its forms— they weren't devoted only to animal sacrifice. They did it with women too, in ways I won't mention here. It began when the city sprang up, but it didn't end when its inhabitants had to abandon it for reasons that will become clear. The wicked man continued to have a taste for meat killed by his own hand, or his own industry.

I, Cain, who had completely lost myself when I struck the blow that killed my brother Abel, in that fury I overcame so long ago and that only rears its head when I remember being with you, Eve. My Eve. Eve, unconditionally ours.

---

9. Rosario Castellanos, "The Rights of the Suicidal," in *Materia memorable* (Mexico City: Universidad Nacional Autónoma de México, 1969).

Eve, so harsh with Cain, my severe mother, merciless only with me. Eve, hard and tender mother. You are my strength, Eve of mine, mother of all mortals, and more my mother than anyone else's.

I, Cain: the farmer who lost my land, the planter condemned to roam, my fortune ill-fated, and ill-fated my change in fortune; because in my wanderings I founded the first city on Earth, in the Land of Nod, condemned, like me, to sterility, and, like me, yearning to be bountiful, fertile, and determined to submit to the Sun, the water, the air, munificent with seeds.

I founded the city thanks to Adah, my love, my sister. I founded Enoch when Adah was with child. Adah expected a child who was ours alone only because my brother had made her with child in violence.

Adah, the mother of Abel's son, the wife of one marked by death, my wife, Cain's woman, pregnant by Abel.

Eve says the giants' children poisoned Enoch to divert our attention from an unbearable scene.

Nod: harsh, rough, cracked, scorching. Nod: steps beyond the salt a fine sand—so soft to the touch, paler than pale, so gentle it was almost pitiful to touch (and made you sad to step on it), like a girl who comes to a man's bed before sprouting breasts, before her torso ends in a nest of fine hairs. Sweetness of sand, and the pain of that sweetness, Nod.

Beyond the sand: gray limestone and thistles, and beyond that, brambles where a variety of blackberries live among bees, spiders, reptiles, and the rapid pecking of colorful birds. A bit farther on: the dark, fertile land (endless and full of hope because it was home to huge birds, flowering shrubs, timid animals, and a bashful spring—hidden between smooth rocks it must have polished with its own effusions—and under the spring, beneath thick reeds, its bubbling sighs), rich, eager to be plowed, yearning constantly for the mysterious and tiny white and ticklish feet of budding roots.

The dark, damp earth opens the tough shells of the seeds with kisses, to coax out the white tips of germinating roots; with these kisses the earth forces seeds to grow stalks, stalks to grow leaves, buds, flowers, the miracle of fruit.

She and I; the Earth and Cain; interwoven, bound together like I was to Eve and Eve to me, because she gave birth to me, and for her I provided fruits, seeds, flour and dough, thread and twine. I was the fertility of Eve's lands. When I lost those first lands, Eve lost me.

Here in Nod, there is no God. Let it be clear, let Adam hear and know that there's no place here for his inventions: Earth gave me fruit because I cultivated the land, because it spoke to me, because it has also been on the lookout, like you, Eve, mother of all peoples, great and gracious, the amiable companion I wished Abel would be. Eve, who was also the source of my anger; but I would never have inflicted it on you, Eve.

The Moon and the Sun are my partners. The water, my soul.

Adah was my joy, until she ceased to be.

Eve the unjust for mating with Adam, the most unjust of all, he of the ill-starred memories. His belly always lacked what he needed to be able to give birth. He's incomplete, as are all of us called men, myself and Abel included, only half human.

Abel and I wanted to correct this. I, with the fertility of my seeds and my vegetables, roots, flowers, fungi, figures carved from wood; and with my hands, which helped Eve with her pottery and the mill and stoking the fire. Abel, with his care for the animals. Abel was less of a fool than I was, when you think about it; he understood our fate better, he played the game Adam's way, with his inheritance of envy and malice.

I was born before you fired the figure of clay.

I, Cain, worked at your side, Eve; I brought everything I had to your hearth, became the master of seeds and fruits to provide you more delightful things to eat. I cooperated, understood, learned; we worked together. My Eve. Naive Eve, you didn't know how to finish what you started between Abel and me, there was no way to fix it, and you planted it, nurtured it, provoked it, cared for it, nourished it, inflamed it. Eve.

Abel was not the only sibling I was close to. Adah will soon give birth to a child who may be female like Adah and Eve, and if she is a girl she may give birth one day, or she may have a barren womb, dark and lightless, and be like me. Barren womb, man-womb, sterile womb. Adah inherited the ability to conceive from Eve. I know others who look like Eve, but they inherited Adam's non-womb. Some are shepherds (like Abel) who kill their animals; two others are like Adah and me, working the land, and the youngest is a potter, like Eve. Only I know how to carve stone.

Adah came with me, though she knew I had lost part of myself when I killed Abel, and that I had been marked by death, wounded by death, wounded like a bee that plants its stinger and ruptures its insides. I had left my stinger in Abel's body too. Death would never come for me because she had already visited me, now she would shun me forevermore. No one would dare try to kill me, nothing could make me die. Nothing and no one, such was the curse of my blood-sin.

And I, the tiller of the soil, I, the founder of the city, I will be condemned to live with the weight of my tomb on my back—part of me died the day Cain died too, like a bee that has stung.

I am not my own worst enemy, nor the least of them. Abel killed everything he raised; all men end up killing what they love. He offered the firstborn of each of his animals in sacrifice—the ones he helped to birth and looked after, as well as the fatted ones. The hands that fed his animals were the same hands that clutched the black stone blade that he used to kill the young. That very idea disgusts Cain. At first it also disgusted Eve, but from that first bleeding throat, and the blood spilling into a bowl that Eve had placed below the wound, Adam drank his fill. Eve tasted the meat, and she approved of it. She used the animals' blood in her cooking. These were the days when I ate my fruits and seeds in the open fields, keeping most of them for myself and Adah. We kept apart from all the others, except Eve.

I made Abel's knife. On the handle Eve inscribed the shape of a feather and the words "goat" and "bee." I also made Eve's knife. On the handle Eve wrote "moon," "dish," and "fire." I made my own knife too, with a plain handle; I could start a fire with it if I struck it against the white stone Eve gave me one day when I was a boy. I didn't make a knife for Adam because I was afraid of him. Today I know that I should have been afraid of Abel, too.

Abel: he made my wife pregnant with a child who poisoned my life, which was already marred by fratricide. (What an unjust fate awaited me; it was my nature to grow, to nurture, to create fertility and life. But death was always waiting for Abel. Death was his, he gave it and gifted it, he sought it out and welcomed it. I fulfilled his desire. He stained my hands with a filthiness that is not mine. I know what he thought when he realized he was wounded: *You'll pay for this, and it gives me joy; you'll be despised forevermore, and it gives me joy; Eve will reject you, and it gives me joy.*)

So said Adam, and then . . . he repeated that Eve had been made from one of his ribs. We all burst out laughing, which upset him. A few days later, after drinking some of the spirits Eve made at home, he lost his mind and started retelling the same story, adding that Yahweh blew the breath of life into him but not into Eve, and then he said that Eve had fallen into the trap of a cunning serpent and the apple blah blah blah, and that her punishment was that she always had to subordinate her desires to his, as did all women to men. He was intoxicated, he had spun his lies into an intoxicating tale which captivated Abel and repulsed us like the stench of a drunkard's breath.

That night Adam took the youngest daughter to his bed. Eve didn't know. I realized when I saw her escape from Adam's hands, her little legs stained with blood.

Let me explain:

Adam, drunk as usual, went to bed and fell asleep as soon as he lay down. The rest of us kept on talking pleasantly while Eve prepared the dough; no one said a word about the tale Adam had just told us. Not even Abel, who always agreed with him; he didn't even mention it.

Abel blurted out he was going to go and check on his animals. "Before I fall asleep, don't anyone set foot in the ostrich pen again." The rest of us went to bed at the same time; I was next to Adah, who had and has my devotion. That night Adah insisted that we sleep next to Eve, to protect her from the evil spirits Adam had awoken.

Adam awoke after the rest of us were sleeping, grabbed our youngest sister, and took her away. She was still a child. I then heard a sound I'd hear many years later, when I set foot on the sands in the Land of Nod.

Weeks later I heard it again, the sound of footsteps on fine sand. The sound came from where Abel was sleeping.

In the Land of Nod, Adah would tell me how, when she was still a child, Adam took her in the broad light of day, soiling her. That time I didn't hear the whispered complaints of the sand.

I killed Abel for Adam's crime. Abel knew this. Evil began with them; they're the ones who begat the cruel evildoers. Eve would come to realize that she had the opportunity to live outside the shadow of those who were cruel thanks to my departure.

Earth decided to poison its waters. It released mercury and arsenic into the springs, poisoning them at the source. We drank rainwater, but it hardly ever rained, and we were always thirsty.

A plague of ants descended. They ate all the plants and devoured cows, dogs, horses, and people indiscriminately.

They were immune to poison. I was left alone, without Adah, without children, without anything to drink. Thirst ruled my days.

Eve will never know that one of my daughters followed the instinct to wander, living in tents, owning livestock, criss-crossing the desert.

Another—and this would have pleased Eve greatly—learned to work with metal. She mined it and forged it, making swords, shields, chains, and other things.

Another daughter of mine observed night-blooming flowers as closely as she observed budding mandarins. She painted them in the colors of night.

One of my sons played the lute, the harp, and the flute, which he made from strong, fragrant wood. The musicians all descended from him.

I myself built the structures where we lived and gathered and bathed. I also designed the plazas and the gardens—or Adah and I did, to be precise.

My life was rich. I had worked and lost the land where I lived with my parents and siblings, sharing it with them. Later, I made mine the land that had been allotted to me as a punishment, because none of my relations lived there, no blood of my blood. I triumphed over my instincts to wander.

Now I am going to die.

I leave you this, my Eve, mother of mine: my curse, which you shall keep as a treasure, because I have made my mark. You shall never die, Eve. That is my legacy to you, and with it I free myself. I am too old. Age will never weigh upon you, because you come from an era where time did not exist; when you sleep the Sun will never subject you to its chronological tyranny. I will live on in you forever, Eve.

ONE ABOUT ABEL:
I, Abel, sought the tree of life in the slaughtered bodies of my animals—my children. Because Eve had children, whereas I reared, nourished, and pastured my animals, and it was good, I called them children, and the children of my children.

I ate them because their flesh was made for me, and it was good.

Pages with the version of another of Eve's daughters

I don't understand a thing. If this story of creation is being told by someone who wants us to love our creator, he's doing his job very poorly. He's working against himself. Let's return to the beginning: the creator speaks to the animals in the language of beasts so as to be understood.

"Everything that grows is made for man to eat." What?

The first thing the creator blesses is the seventh day. Damn; idleness, and everything is frozen in place.

And he hadn't even made it rain upon the land. So how could the plants have grown?

He's a murderer. "And God saw that it was good"—all the animals he had created in the sea and in the air. Weren't they even worth eating? He killed them just for the sake of it? Which brings me to the story of Cain and Abel, but I won't digress.

I won't hurry on too quickly, though, because why would he have created creatures that crawled and slithered and then said that crawling and slithering was a punishment, imposed harshly upon the serpents?

Let's leave that aside. They say that he created the animals in his own image and likeness—which covers a broad spectrum, from the mandrill to the spider—and gave them all one common feature: all had both males and females. Hmmm, was that in his image and likeness? Males and females? Was the creator bisexual? Without a doubt. That makes me feel better . . . a little bit.

Because the passage in which Adam and the woman experience shame comes almost immediately after that. They make clothes out of fig leaves. When the creator intervenes, he dresses them in animal skins. Let's see, shouldn't we pause a moment? Is it really the same to dress—cover up—in plants as it is to do so in parts of dead animals? Perhaps, but I say absolutely not. I accept the argument, but I disagree. How? The creator extravagantly slaughtered what he had just made? Or had death already become a necessary part of life? Genesis doesn't say. He killed to clothe them.

Which explains his reaction to the Cain and Abel affair. Cain was a farmer and, we can assume, a vegetarian; but even if he hadn't left the family home, he was a carnivore by association. Abel, on the other hand, was a butcher. The smoke of the animal fat he offered to the creator is evidence that he didn't just lay his hands on animals that died naturally, but that he murdered them. He was both shepherd and butcher—he had to be both because there were so few people in the world back then.

People who suddenly multiplied, with no logical explanation. How did Cain wed? Where in the universe did these women that he mated with suddenly appear from?

The only logical explanation that makes sense is that they were giantesses. Which would explain a lot of things: their revulsion to women, misogyny, and enduring resentment. How can you get along with a giantess if you're a dwarf in her eyes?

Consider a world peopled by the progeny of these giantess wives and descendants of the vegetarian, Cain . . .

Pages from Another One of Eve's Daughters

Eve always changes the truth, insisting upon her version. What she has told us is incorrect. This is the truth:

Leviathan was born in Eden, early on, like moss. He sprang up. Nothing could stop him. He was the most stubborn of creatures. The Creator noticed this and took action. Leviathan had to be eliminated. But Leviathan was too quick. He had a female companion, made from nothingness, like him. The Creator didn't want to kill her; he wanted to know her. But he realized that he was not worthy of her, and this fact was unbearable. So he killed her. He only castrated Leviathan, which literally neutralized him, and it was the perfect revenge.

Their conflict didn't end there. One day the Creator and Leviathan were destined to battle hand to hand, it was dreadful. For this occasion, the Creator prepared a brine from the flesh of Leviathan's lovely wife. He made two coats from her skin. And dressed Adam and Eve in them when they were expelled from Paradise.

The coats shone like fish scales. Resplendent, iridescent coats. More beautiful than the dead creature was when she was alive. Thus dressed, Eve and her companion went out into the world.

What I'm telling you is the truth. Everything else was whipped up by Eve.

There's one thing I'd like to add. The skin of Leviathan's wife smelled like him; it gave off an unbearable, disgusting stench. Which is why Leviathan took as many flowers as he could from Paradise, trying to capture their scent.

The skin of the victim had no way hide in the perfume of flowers; it couldn't move, and it couldn't even feel. Like Leviathan, it reeked of pestilence. It would have liked to be among flowers and let their perfume penetrate it.

The destiny of flowers is inevitably awful. Exposed by their design, they must give of their intimate essence to that which is pestilent, born of death, repugnant. Therein lies their fate, to make hypocrites and sycophants look and smell good. They lost their purpose by fulfilling their destiny. That's why flowers are nothing more than short-lived promises. Intrinsic lies. Pretty, yes. Sweet-smelling too. But they're not masks or shields, and they can't cover up bad odors. They show us that they won't last. They're the tools of impostors.

What's worse: the pickled beauty wouldn't be the only dish served at the banquet celebrating the Creator's victory over Leviathan. After great battles, many victors consume the flesh of their victims, pronouncing it delicious. But there's one last thing. One more dish to be served; but one of my sisters will have to tell of that.

BOOK NINE

76

Enoch in Nod

A singular vision awaited me: Enoch, the city founded by Cain. The city wall was my first surprise (we hadn't ever built stone walls); it was so magnificent, symmetrical, and strange, so of-the-desert, so reflective of light. Then there was the orderliness of the streets and buildings, the wells surrounded by gardens, the marketplace—extraordinary—and so very many people.

And up above, a starry sky—each star seemingly connected to the next. It was what it was, designed for tranquility, unlike the world. Every corner had its own delights. The people passing by—who numbered many—wore clothes I had never seen and moved so differently.

In the market I asked for something to eat. We didn't use what they called money, but out of respect for their elders they attended to old Eve and accepted one of my animals in return for food for me and my creatures. They offered me a table right there, so I sat down and a young man (who was really a boy, though he lowered his voice to sound more mature) took the reins of my animals and looked after them, giving them to eat and to drink, and finding them shade to rest.

While I ate from a beautiful ceramic plate, which hardly looked anything like my own—the ones I made with Adah and Cain—I asked if someone could tell me what had become of Cain.

A seed vendor who carried a burlap sack around his neck was eager to speak (in the city so many people were alone) and he told me that, after killing his brother, Cain grew a kind of horn between his eyebrows; that he suffered from the shakes constantly, like the leaves of a tree in the wind, even when he slept, which is perhaps why he found it difficult to sleep and hardly ever did; that he was always hungry no matter how much he ate; that he was cursed and had no friends. And that without a doubt he had founded the city when Enoch, his firstborn, arrived, followed by six others: Mauli, Leeth, Teze, Iesca, Celeth, and Tebbath.

Someone else passing by (without wares for sale) said that if Cain had founded Enoch, it was purely out of vanity, as a monument to himself. That he had built walls around all six cities he founded. That he was a thief. That Cain only thought about himself, which is why he created weights and measures and money. That he had fought with his brother Abel even in his mother's womb, and that he was good at fighting and causing disaster.

A woman told me that Cain had tried to bury Abel before leaving home, after he was cursed by his father, but that Earth wouldn't accept his brother because she was still angry about the dust that had been stolen from her to make Adam.

The more they told me about Cain, the less I recognized my son, the tiller of the soil, in their stories. And in these stories, I heard faint echoes of Adam's stories, which intrigued me further.

A blind man was the only one who noticed my confusion. He sat down beside me and, changing the subject slightly, he told me the following story:

77

The Story of Lamech

It happened that the grandchild of one of Cain's grandchildren, called Lamech, preferred to spend his days outside of Enoch. He was a hunter, and a clever one. He lived a long life in this way, in the open air, without shade, seeking the quarry that he sold at market once he had butchered it. This life in the sun slowly ruined his sight until he went blind. Even then he had no interest in spending his days within the city walls: he bought one of his grandsons from one of his sons (and changed the boy's name to Tubal-Cain) and trained him to act as his own eyes, which was the only thing he lacked to continue hunting. He told the boy to call him grandfather.

One day when they were out hunting, Tubal-Cain pulled on Lamech's robes in a way that meant (according to their code), *Look, Grandfather, straight ahead about seventeen paces away I see the golden hair of a beast rising in the brush. Now's the moment, hurry!* Lamech drew his bow, aimed precisely, and hit his target. Tubal-Cain ran to bring back their prey. When he reached it, he yelled, "Grandfather, you've just killed a man! Your arrow went straight through his neck. He must have been a terrible man because he has an awful mark on his brow! A horn growing out of his forehead!"

"Alas! Woe betide me! I have killed immortal Cain!"

And Lamech wrung his hands in grief over what he had just done, and since he was still holding his bow and arrows, he accidentally shot one off, wounding the boy mortally. He heard the arrow fly. He went over to Cain. His hands felt the two fallen bodies and so great was his grief that he lay down in that place to await death, weeping and shouting, "May I and all of my progeny be cursed! A thousand times cursed since I have killed mine own eyes and my boy both with one shot!"

When night fell both his wives became worried about his absence, so, accompanied by their sons, they went to look for Tubal-Cain and Lamech; they found two corpses and one more dying of grief. When he heard them coming, Lamech began to weep and moan again, adding, "Give me solace! Come lie with me! Perhaps if I mate with you, I will feel worthy of life once more!"

Both wives refused. Zillah ruled the roost: "You have killed our grandfather Cain and you have murdered my son Tubal-Cain! How could we lie with you now? Don't be disgusting! Don't make us despise you more!"

"Do what I say! I am your husband! You shall do my bidding! I'm the one who gives the orders here!"

Then Ara replied, "You're revolting to both of us. You have killed our child and our grandfather."

But then the two wives looked at each other and though they felt revulsion they lay with him out of foolishness and pity, each helping the other. And so, Zillah got with child. He was called Noah, and he was just.

Others said that Noah was not their child, that what happened was that Earth felt their revulsion, opened up, and swallowed all of them up out of sympathy.

At the end of this story the blind man asked the woman who had provided my meal if she could bring an apple for Eve courtesy of him.

I looked at it; it bore no resemblance to the fruit in Paradise. I bit it. Its crunch was exactly like the one I ate in Eden, identical. But its flavor was different, although it was trying to be the same.

It is because of this fruit that Cain believed the fruit in Eden was called an "apple."

78

What Became of Cain and Adah

In the market I asked after Adah and her children. No one knew a thing about her. "Cain had two wives, like all the men," was the only thing I was able to learn. "And here, sons belong to their fathers, so we can tell you with certainty that all of Cain's sons are dead. And we know that his grandsons are dead, too."

"And Cain's daughters?"

"Here the daughters don't belong to anyone. Male offspring are acknowledged; a good daughter marries well, and that's the end of it."

And no matter how well she marries, I thought to myself, *she'll only be half married, if each man has two wives.*

79

Who Was Noah, Really?

I heard different versions of Noah's birth. The one that interested me the most held that his father didn't recognize him as his own child, thinking that he had come from some other seed. Noah's father rejected him. But there was proof (I don't know what, no one wanted to go into detail for me) that his son really was his son, so in the end Cain's grandson accepted him. This story endeared Noah to me. And the blind man told me more:

"Earth changed for the better with the birth of Noah and the death of Cain; she became more generous. Healthy wheat sprouted. This was when Cain got one of the grafted trees to grow an apple, in the likeness of Eve's."

I'm not sure he was telling me the truth. And if it were true, was it the appearance of an angel or a devil or a giant that made the tree in Eden produce the fruit that brought us here?

80

More about Noah

These stories they told me piqued my interest in Noah. There are other versions I won't include here. Now I'll tell you everything I know about him firsthand, and why.

I was old, without family, and unknown to everyone since Cain was dead and no one knew who I was because I couldn't find a way to explain without making a fool of myself trying—who would believe me? And I understood that in Nod people claimed ownership over their plots of land (Really?? Plots of land with owners?!), which made it impossible for me to find a place to pitch my tent and stay. So, not wishing to lose my animals one by one in exchange for meals and gossip, I found a Noddite who would pasture my animals for a monthly fee (in his currency). I also needed money to buy food for myself and a place to sleep (it was impossible to lie down and rest anywhere in their noisy streets).

So I went in search of work, though I wasn't in urgent need. I had various options and chose the one that seemed most appealing.

81

With Noah, His So-Called Flood and Ark

I began to work for Noah as his cook. He had heard my story (just what the townspeople knew: that I had arrived aged and alone in my skiff, accompanied only by my animals) and he wanted someone who wasn't from Nod to prepare his food. And he was accustomed to eating well, just as I was accustomed to cooking well (it's not my fault, it's the apple's).

Having heard about Noah's proverbial rectitude (about him it was written, "God loved this man for his rectitude"), I could never have imagined what awaited me when I accepted.

My experience in my boat had been most pleasant. I had enjoyed a sense of immense freedom—traveling adrift in that swollen river was intoxicating—and it wasn't that I was seeking a similar pleasure; I just thought that the hearth and the kitchen would give me back the joy that had disappeared when I lost my flock to Adam's nonsense. Noah told me I could cook whatever I liked.

Shut in a dark room with rough wooden walls where it was always damp, since the house's well was directly below, I was subjected to abuse by all of them; more than once Noah's sons came down to manhandle me, playing with me in the darkness, not because they wanted new flesh (they already had their wives) but just for the thrill of mistreating a good woman. My clitoris became timid and cowardly, mostly due to Noah. He chose to behave as the others; he was a man to be feared, given to drunkenness—which is why they say he was intoxicated when he left the ark. The truth is that his rectitude was twisted this way and that—in his imagination, for a start.

Because it turned out that Noah, whose food I served, decided to steal the story of my voyage to Enoch, announcing that he had been chosen by God to be the only survivor of a great flood, and that because he was the most righteous of men, the ark and all the others, etcetera, you know the story.

First Adam stole the true story of our origins. Then Noah did it again. Story thieves.

And there in his tale, in his imagination, he said that he brought his three sons and their wives aboard the ark with him. Could you call Noah a man of rectitude, one who believed his actions were right and just, if he left his daughters to drown in the flood?

The reality is that not only did he steal my story, Noah was extremely strict and intolerant with his sons. Shem was the eldest, followed by Ham, and the youngest was Japheth. When he wasn't strict, he was arbitrary. One example of his unfairness:

His youngest son, Ham, was thrown out of the house because he accidentally saw master Noah naked one night when he had gotten drunk and taken off his clothes. Does that punishment make any sense? Is it not absurd, arbitrary, and excessive? Noah punished Ham for his own weakness; Ham paid for his father's mistake.

There's more about Noah, the imagination-thief of my boat. He was constantly terrified, which caused him to make the most horrific sacrifices. Fear nested deep in his heart, eating away at him like a colony of red ants. In real life, and in the story that he concocted out of mine, he said that when the great flood was over and the water finally receded, he saw the dove and the olive branch as a dreadful sign. Since the dove was covered in mud, he thought that it was no longer a bird that could fly weightlessly above our heads, but rather a creature that had to drag itself along the ground like a snake. Likewise, the olive branch was not a sign of hope but a threat: if the storm returned, the olive tree would be inundated and die, and this time—since it no longer bore any fruit because it hadn't had enough time to produce any—it would be dead forever. In sum, he saw a serpent in the dove and death in the olive branch. Those who retold his story changed it and gave the dove and the olive branch different meanings using basic common sense, since their vision was not blinded by fear. But they didn't put Noah's daughters in his ark.

All three of his sons—I don't forgive any of them—made that dark and damp kitchen a prison sentence of constant abuse. Later, when they couldn't put up with Noah and longer, they moved away, leaving the mountains behind, and settling in the valleys.

But I was going to tell you about how the anxiety and fear that dogged Noah caused him to do abominable things, calling them "sacrifices" in his eagerness to satisfy the whims of his god. These were the sacrifices Noah made to pacify his creator: corporal punishment, butchering newborn animals, enslaving and trading them, branding them with fire, and relegating women to silence.

Noah's home stank of blood and death.

82

Escaping from Noah

Let's forget this period of imprisonment in his stifling kitchen: there was hardly even room for a cook there. I ran away in the middle of the night when everyone was sleeping, afraid that Noah would wake up, because several hours earlier he had fallen into one of his deep alcoholic slumbers, lying not far from the door. (We never carried him to his bed because it infuriated him to awaken in our hands. And then we also had to deal with drunken Noah's erections.) I had no desire to add to the race of cripples Noah's women had borne him; his seed was always groggy from alcohol when it entered the female womb.

So, I fled by night to avoid being whipped if they caught me. I walked for days. I came to a broad, clear plain. It had two advantages: there was fresh water to drink, and it was full of small fish and crustaceans, with thick, sweet grass growing on its banks. There were some trees with sturdy trunks but nothing else. I made a fire, covered myself with the blanket, one of my few remaining possessions, and lay down to sleep in the open air.

END OF BOOK NINE

BOOK TEN

83

Eve Alone on the Plain

For years I was alone, companionless, my body the only refuge for my memories. I wasn't consumed by grief as I had been on past occasions, but joy didn't visit me either. I lived in remembrance and in this way, I attained a sort of immortality. It didn't occur to me to stop, despite the fact my life was a state of limbo, though melancholy kept track of the days.

What follows here is what I heard when the mob found my sanctuary, bringing this phase of my life to an end. I'll tell it exactly as it was told to me, though I can't be certain whether or not it happened:

84

Noah Divides the Land, Creating Princes

After my departure, Noah, who was widely esteemed and respected (thanks to my journey in the ark, which he stole from me and tainted with his innate fear of a great flood), began acquiring land until he owned every corner of Earth and proceeded to gather his three sons to divide the land between them. He had drawn the borders of these properties on three scrolls of papyrus. He wished to leave to chance the choice of which son got which lot; he asked an angel to be present to witness his impartiality.

Shem was the first to take a scroll from Noah's lap. He got the best portion—the nearest lands, which were known to be fertile. Noah was well pleased. Shem would have Mount Sinai, Mount Zion, and the Holy Temple, which they believed was the center of the Earth; the climate there was ideal—not too hot and not too cold. The hot south fell to Ham—the youngest of the sons, the one Noah had thrown out for seeing him unclothed—and the frigid north to Japheth. As soon as they received their lots, Noah's sons divided their property among their own children. And in front of the Angel Noah declared, "Cursed be the one who attempts to steal a portion of land that has not been allotted to him by my law." And his sons accepted this pronouncement: "So shall it be, so shall it be."

The land remained divided. Earth now worked seventy-two times harder for her owners, and in each nation there were 140 lots and ninety-one islands. I want to make it clear that not a single woman owned any of this. That each of Noah's numerous descendants had wives and daughters who had no rights to ownership and who were, like the Earth, slaves to their fathers or husbands.

The stories Adam invented had triumphed. And therein lies the power of the word: it shapes mankind, their customs, their communities. Words don't just say things, they do things.

But Earth is not an obedient slave. Nine-tenths of the men became very sick. The Angel Raphael (who I believe is a demon) gifted Noah some remedies for his ailments, and Noah noted the instructions down carefully. That became the first medical handbook. But the remedies weren't strong enough; across the nations, magicians, astrologers, and wise men applied themselves to finding a cure, trying with trees, flowers, earth, burning and drying plants and powders, making poultices, tinctures, and perfumes. The ingenuity of the Angel and the peoples conquered this illness, and the men recovered completely.

However, the survivors had damaged, unhealthy hearts. And they knew that if they harbored resentment about the way the land had been cut up like a cake at their own party, they would have been punished. They designated a prince in each country and worshipped them like idols, bringing them offerings and making them tributes, making themselves slaves to the ones they had placed in power. Only twelve men refused to worship one of these princes, and they were all burned at the stake. Their ashes were rejected by the Earth because they too had enslaved her.

85

Nimrod

A king was appointed to oversee the twelve princes: Nimrod. He claimed to have the hides in which "God" (who was no longer called Thunder, or the "unnameable," or even referred to as the Creator) had dressed Adam and me when we left Eden. Nimrod said the hides had been inside Noah's imaginary ark. I knew everything that had been aboard my own boat and can testify (because I know without a doubt) that they were not on that boat either; unless he was referring to my own skin, the only skin that traveled in the ark and had once been in Eden, Nimrod was lying.

"Whoever dons these hides," Nimrod decreed, "is invincible and irresistible." He did win battles in them, subjugating the princes and their flocks of men and all their slave women. Nimrod said that the birds and all the beasts of the forests revered him too—but he lived within city walls and had no way of proving that the animals of the forests, deserts, or seas had any respect for him whatsoever.

Nimrod said that his stone and wooden idols conferred great power upon him. He was indisputably a ruthless warrior who obtained his power by force, theft, and of course storytelling and other lies.

In short, he declared he was God. He had a throne of cedar made atop a boulder and atop this he placed four more thrones: one of copper, one of iron, one of silver, and, at the top, one of gold.

And crowning all these thrones a giant round gemstone atop the golden throne. It was upon this gemstone that Nimrod sat, while the princes and their courtiers paid their respects and asked for his protection like so many retinues of wretches.

It was Nimrod's idea to build a capital city on an uninhabited plateau, as a representation of humanity's might.

86

The Arrival of Nimrod's Hordes
and Nimrod's Decree

And so, Noah's descendants began walking eastward until they arrived upon the plain where I was living. There was nothing out of the ordinary about that place, it was just flat, solid land covered with grass—an open space.

I had been alone so long that, at first, I was overjoyed to hear the multitude approaching. Then I began to worry that since I wasn't one of their own, they might try to harm me. Since they were humans, the fire wouldn't keep them at a distance. I decided to hide behind a tree and as soon as they came close, I slipped into the crowd, pretending to be one of them.

87

The Tower of Babel and Our Great Dream

In the center of the city that they were about to start building they planned to erect a tower so tall it would reach Heaven. Stone was not good for this, so they used oven-fired bricks, which were lighter and could be easily shaped, making them ideal for buildings of any dimension.

We began to work. Thousands of us had united in this common cause. Meals were prepared in the open air, and some people slept between their bundles of belongings. Eager to accomplish their goal, they lived in a state of disarray.

No one escaped the tyranny of the long days. Guards patrolled the part of the plain that had been settled to ensure that no one was shirking work. We all had to pitch in for the construction; most of us participated willingly, possessed by this dream. The guards didn't need to use force thanks to the collective fervor.

I offered to make the bread (in the ovens that fired the bricks) and I distributed it daily; I also helped make the bricks.

When night fell, everyone was exhausted; we women prepared the meal with whatever had been sent from the markets in the cities in the nations of Noah's sons. We didn't use money, so everyone received the same size portion on their plate. The men kept silent, resting, while we women wove stories together. But not about our origins—we didn't try to reestablish the true version that would have set us all free; we too had become obsessed with the Great Tower.

"We'll go up to Heaven and wage war on everyone who's living up there, where they have enough food, it's never too hot or too cold, and they lack for nothing. Let's make war on the citizens of Heaven!"

And the ones who were saying this launched arrows into the sky, some claiming that they fell back down to Earth with bloody tips, but I didn't see any.

"Let's go up to Heaven and set up our own idols and worship them there."

"To Heaven! Why is it that the god who lives there is the only one entitled to live above the Earth? God has no right to make a home on high while we're stuck down below. When we get there let's erect a monument to our achievements. We're just as good as the ones up there are! We want to be where we can see everything and hear everything, no one can hide from us, and we can be the masters of Earth."

"To Heaven! To Heaven! If we make our tower high enough, we'll reach the Moon. We'll conquer the skies!"

There were those who, fearful as Noah, participated in the construction of the Tower because they were afraid that there would be another great flood. The building would save them from the floodwaters. They were no less zealous.

Everyone was possessed by the same fanatical zeal.

Their fervor also infected me. I don't know if there was anyone among us who didn't feel it.

Once a considerable store of bricks had been fired and many gallons of tar had been stockpiled, we began to build the tower. We held it in our hearts, determined to succeed. It was our priority, our obsession; before building the walls of our kitchens or bedrooms we wanted to complete this tower that would be so tall it would touch the sky.

We worked hard at building it for a long time. We wanted to make it so tall that it would take a year to reach the top.

While we were building, people didn't matter nearly as much as the bricks, which were more valuable than anything else. If someone fell, what did it matter in the grand scheme of things? Individuals were meaningless; more than a hundred thousand of us worked on the tower, and at least half of them were women. Pregnant women, girls, boys, old women and old men, everyone participated in the great project. Who cared about a woman in childbirth, compared to a finished wall? If an infant peeked out between her legs while she was pushing and bathed in sweat, the difficult work of brickmaking did not stop, because the bricks were much more important than the newborn; someone would give the newborn a thin blanket provided by the organization—a triangle of fabric that served as both a diaper and a blanket, which was practical: napkin, swaddling, and blanket all in one.

Down below no one gathered up the fallen bodies, the cadavers' teeth bared to the open air.

Of course, the birds of the plain could no longer reach us, we were so high up.

It was a source of group pride. The tower belonged to everyone. Cain's idea of building walls and dividing the land among individuals had been cast aside; the tower belonged to all of us. We were all equals! We also stopped the Cainite use of money, but we did employ measures and weights because we needed to use them to ensure that our tower would stand; no single wall could weigh more than another.

Now, was this tower anything but a dream? What would we use it for? Where would children play? Where would meals be prepared? Where would people make love? These questions went unanswered. Everyone was united in this group effort, which roused feelings of pride and satisfaction at being a part of something Together.

—

The determination and perseverance of Noah's many children, grandchildren, and great grandchildren built that high tower. It had countless windows and later we improvised places where the community could gather for fun, refresh themselves, and even sleep for a few minutes. During that time, we slept wherever we were working when night fell and awoke at dawn to begin anew. A human chain delivered a little food to eat and something to drink. Pride kept us going; it really was a perfect structure. Along the top of the tower there was a street; the tower was like an open city with a spiral staircase from the bottom to the top.

We thought it wasn't important to be able use the inside of the tower except as a final resting place. It remained to be seen how that might be accomplished; for the time being it was build, build, build that formidably high, hollow tower.

Built entirely of brick and a little tar, it continued ascending into the sky until those who were opposed to it intervened:

88

Opposition to the Tower

The giants and the demons, Thunder (Adam's unnameable god), and everything else that wasn't human joined forces to shatter Nimrod's plan. "They'll take over every inch of the Earth and consume everything if we let them, and we'll be left with nothing more to rule over." Earth was even angrier. What she had known from the beginning was proving true: the hordes of humanity would strip her bare. Arrogant, they continued to build upon her surface, ignoring her. And if there were thousands now, there would eventually be millions and billions and trillions; every square inch of her would be populated.

Since she was the angriest, she decided to take action. It was easy: all she needed to do was jump and tremble a little, just for three minutes.

When we finished the tenth staircase to Heaven, the zeal for our Great Plan grew; we were sure that we would reach Heaven. The archers were launching more and more arrows, and those who exhorted us to keep on working never ceased urging us on.

Night fell upon us, along with exhaustion; suddenly, Earth began to shake and jump and vibrate constantly.

Earth's leap made about half the ground the tower stood upon rise six cubits, right down its center. The other half sank two cubits lower, sliding down unevenly in the middle and rising again to its original height at the perimeter.

The irony is that we chose the place where we built the tower because it was perfectly flat. After the earthquake it was impossible to find any stretch of land that was more absurdly uneven and steep in places.

It goes without saying that the walls came crumbling down—first the ones closest to the ground, which made the ones resting atop them tumble down too, and so on and so forth, as rapidly as if they were drops of rain. The people who were working at the top were smashed to pieces and those who were working down below were crushed by everyone and everything that fell on top of them. The only people we could see had landed atop this terrestrial debacle, crowning the rubble; their bones were broken and they couldn't even gnash their teeth.

89

Surviving Babel. The New Cain

When the Tower of Babel crumbled so violently and quickly, the few survivors of the impassioned multitude (who had been working together like a fine-tuned machine just moments before) stampeded away from that cursed place.

For a long time, I believed I was alone among the rubble. I didn't want to run away. I contemplated the scene without fully comprehending what had happened, what this ruin of bricks really was.

The only sound was the shifting of the ruined building as it continued to fall and settle, like a dying animal.

Most of us had been working at the top, preparing to carry more bricks even higher, but there were also a number of people carrying blocks, tar, water, and food upward, and more people descending with empty hands only to repeat the journey back up again. There wasn't so much as a moan from any of them. They had become one with the wreckage. Thousands of cadavers lay beneath the walls that had been dashed to pieces, which now formed misshapen mounds of debris with jagged peaks and steep ravines.

In the cloud of brown dust that the collapse had created I observed a figure moving and then another one a little farther off. They were women, dazed like I was. One was desperately searching for her children in the rubble—"Even if I find the two who were here in the tower, they were just infants"; the second was searching for her sisters—"We left Enoch together, and together we'll return." I helped them look.

That's what we were doing when we heard a deafening thunderclap; even Thunder couldn't have made such a sound. It was spectacularly loud, hurting our ears and striking fear in our hearts. It came from the East. We ran in the opposite direction, away from what seemed to be a much greater danger. The sky lit up with a brilliant bolt of lightning as if echoing the roar that continued to rumble. At my feet I saw the body of a boy who couldn't have been more than eleven years old, if that. He was facedown. I touched him. His arm was warm, and his pulse beat with life. I shook him to wake him up. The bright thunderbolt gave me the seconds I needed to roll him onto his back; I saw his face, which had a horn between the eyebrows, just like Cain had been described to me. The boy opened his eyes. I pulled him upright. His legs sprang to life and he began to run, leaning on me for the first few steps, but then suddenly he was pulling me along vigorously.

The rumbling ceased. Then we heard the sound of water rushing. Thinking we were doomed, we scrambled up an enormous tree beside us. The boy and the younger woman scaled it quickly like leopards.

Another thunderbolt struck. The tree had holes in its trunk where the other woman and I put our feet to climb it; we reached our companions. The four of us huddled together, lodged in the thick tangle of branches at the treetop.

The tree trunk withstood the torrent of water that was rushing across the plain. Earth's movement had altered the course of some river or burst the banks of a neighboring lake.

Dawn broke like a fine thread along the length of night's horizon.

Dead bodies floated in the water.

A torrential rain began, violently reshaping the lumpen mountains of brick. More bodies floated to the surface. None of them showed the least sign of life. It looked like some invisible hand had placed them side by side, because all of them—children, men, women, the elderly, the young—floated facedown. None of them had wings on their back.

The Earth bucked again, terrifying us. We wrapped ourselves around a thick branch with our arms and our legs. Earth rumbled more loudly than the thunder but more quietly than the water invading the plain.

Then Earth bucked once more, making a huge sighing sound that was almost human.

The water drained into the Earth and disappeared. The plain was wet but no longer flooded, and it wasn't much of a plain anymore. Where the impossibly high tower had once stood, the Earth had swallowed everything: the water, the bodies floating in it, and what remained of the building.

A third movement, a trembling. Something that looked like tar or asphalt erupted from the place Earth had swallowed everything, creating a little lake that wasn't even half the size of the perimeter of the tower. And silence fell. And the Sun came out. And everything looked impossibly peaceful. We sat on our branch. Our breath became calmer. In this stillness, the boy with the mark of Cain spoke:

"What happened? I fell asleep before taking another load to the top of the tower, and then you woke me up, lady. Where did the tower go?"

I wanted to explain in a way that he would understand—an earthquake, the Earth's anger, Babel. But I couldn't get a word out.

—

We climbed down the tree. The first woman, the one I had observed walking through the ruins like a shadow, ran to the water. Fearless—she was looking for her children—she began wading through the water, which was no deeper than half a cubit.

We three women and the boy took a few steps in the water, slipping on the tar, until we came to our senses and got out of the water, which was draining into the deepest parts of the ground, leaving behind nothing but tar residue. We moved away before the Earth devoured us too.

90

Eve Wonders

The dream, the Great Project, collapsed along with the tower. The scales fell from my eyes: where had I been when I was carrying bricks? What had I become, invested in the dream of that zealous mob? I had seen my fellow beings fall and I had ignored them, my senses clouded by the communal delusion of being Great by building something great to defeat the powers in Heaven.

91

Eve's Laughter

Young Cain's hands sow our crops. The four of us are weaving a tent out of papyrus. We build fires. We make lamps from tar, plates from clay, combs from wood, knives from bone, a flute and strings for making music. We sing. We dance. Of course, we dream every night, but we struggle to tell each other about them—people can't be replaced by bricks, though in nightmares they sometimes are.

If anyone were to visit, they would have to walk through the desert and would be surprised to discover this green garden, our home.

Are we the only survivors? If there are others, do they speak another language? Do they see the world differently? If they do, so much the better, because it will help prevent Nimrodian ambition from flourishing once more.

It's not always true that he who laughs last laughs hardest.

One day the Moon laughed and her laughter scarred Earth's body. I don't know if anyone remembers this, but I do know that it happened.

Listen carefully now because I'm the one laughing. I don't know if I'm laughing the hardest. I do know I'm alive. Accompanied by two women and a new son—whom I didn't give birth to but who I know is the flesh of my flesh, my descendant; and I'm the one saying, as Cain once did, "life is good." The world begins anew.

END OF THE BOOK OF EVE

Carmen Boullosa is one of Mexico's leading novelists. She has published twenty novels, four of which are available in English from Deep Vellum. Boullosa has received numerous prizes and honors, including a Guggenheim fellowship. Also a poet, playwright, essayist, and cultural critic, Boullosa is a distinguished lecturer at City College of New York, and her books have been translated into Italian, Dutch, German, French, Portuguese, Chinese, and Russian. Other novels translated into English include *Before* (tr. Peter Bush, Deep Vellum, 2016), *Heavens On Earth* (tr. Shelby Vincent, Deep Vellum, 2017), and *The Book of Anna* (tr. Samantha Schnee, Coffee House Press, 2020).

Samantha Schnee is a 2023 recipient of the National Endowment for the Arts Literature Fellowship in Translation, supporting her work to render Boullosa's Café Gijón Prize–winning novel, *El complot de los Románticos*, into English as *Dante Hits the Road*. Her translation of Boullosa's *Texas: The Great Theft* (Deep Vellum, 2014) was short-listed for the PEN America Translation Prize. She is the founding editor of *Words Without Borders*.

CPSIA information can be obtained
at www.ICGtesting.com
Printed in the USA
JSHW081801140723
44790JS00003B/4